JACK of SPADES

JACK of SPADES

Also by Joyce Carol Oates

JACK of SPADES

JACK of SPADES

A TALE OF SUSPENSE

JOYCE CAROL OATES

The Mysterious Press
an imprint of Grove/Atlantic, Inc.
New York

Published simultaneously in Canada
Printed in the United States of America

FIRST EDITION

ISBN 978-0-8021-2394-7
eISBN 978-0-8021-9103-8

The Mysterious Press
an imprint of Grove Atlantic
154 West 14th Street
New York, NY 10011

Distributed by Publishers Group West

groveatlantic.com

15 16 17 18   10 9 8 7 6 5 4 3 2 1

For Otto Penzler

We stand upon the brink of a precipice. We peer into the abyss—
we grow sick and dizzy. Our first impulse is to shrink from the
danger. Unaccountably we remain.

Edgar Allan Poe, "The Imp of the Perverse"

I

1   The Ax

Out of the air, the ax. Somehow there was an ax and it rose
and fell in a wild swath aimed at my head even as I tried to
rise from my squatting position and lost my balance desperate to escape as my legs faltered beneath me and there came a
hoarse pleading voice—"No! No please! No"—(was this my
own choked voice, unrecognizable?)—as the ax-blade crashed
and sank into the splintering desk beside my head missing my
head by inches; by which time I'd fallen heavily onto the floor,
a hard unyielding floor beneath the frayed Oriental carpet. I
was scrambling to right myself, grabbing for the ax, desperate
to seize the ax, in the blindness of desperation my hands flailing, and the voice (my own? my assailant's?) high-pitched and
hardly human-sounding—"No! *Nooo*"—a fleeting glimpse of
the assailant's stubby fingers and dead-white ropey-muscled
arms inside the flimsy sleeves of nightwear, and a grunting
cry as of triumph and fury commingled; and again the terrible
lifting of the ax-head, the dull sheen of the crude ax-blade,

and the downward swing of Death once begun unstoppable, irretrievable plunging into a human skull as easily rent as a melon with no more protection than a thick rind, to expose the pulpy gray-matter of the brain amid a torrential gushing of arterial blood.

And still the voice rising disbelieving *No no no no no.*

2 "Jack of Spades"

Five months, two weeks and six days before, it had begun in-nocently. There was no reason to suspect that "Jack of Spades" would be involved at all.

For no one here in Harbourton knew about "Jack of Spades"—even now, no one knows. Not one person who is close to Andrew J. Rush—my parents, my wife and children, neighbors, longtime friends of mine from high school.

Here, in this rural-suburban community in New Jersey where I was born fifty-three years ago, and where I have lived with my dear wife, Irina, for more than seventeen years, I am known as "Andrew J. Rush"—arguably the most famous of local residents, author of bestselling mystery-suspense novels with a touch of the macabre. (Not an excessive touch, not nasty-mean, or dis-turbing. Never obscene, nor even sexist. Women are treated graciously in my mysteries, apart from a few obligatory *noir* performances. Corpses are likely to be white adult males.) With my third bestseller in the 1990s it began to be said about me in the media—*Andrew J. Rush is the gentleman's Stephen King.*

Of course, I was flattered. Sales of my novels, though in the millions after a quarter-century of effort, are yet in the double-digit millions and not the triple-digit, like Stephen King's. And though my novels have been translated into as many as thirty languages—(quite a surprise to me, who knows only one language)—I'm sure that Stephen King's books have been translated into even more, and more profitably. And only three of my novels have been adapted into (quickly forgotten) films, and only two into (less-than-premium cable) TV dramas—unlike King, whose adaptations are too many to count.

So far as money is concerned, there is no comparing Andrew J. Rush and Stephen King. But when you have made, after taxes, somewhere in excess of thirty million dollars, you simply stop thinking about *money,* as, perhaps, a serial killer simply stops thinking about how many people he has killed, after a few dozen victims.

(Excuse me! I think that must have been a callous remark, which I'm sure would provoke my dear Irina to kick my ankle in reprimand as she sometimes does when I misspeak in public. *I did not mean to be callous at all* but only just "witty"—in my clumsy way.)

However flattered I was by the comparison to Stephen King, I refused to allow my publisher to use this statement on the dust jacket of my next novel without first seeking permission from King; my admiration for Stephen King—(yes, and my envy of him)—didn't blind me to the possibility that such a statement might be offensive to him, as well as exploitative. But

Stephen King didn't seem to care in the slightest. Reportedly he'd just laughed—*Who'd want to be the gentleman's Stephen King, anyway?*

(Was this a condescending remark from a literary legend, tantamount to brushing away an annoying fly, or just a good-natured rejoinder from a fellow writer? As Andrew J. Rush is himself a good-natured individual, I chose to believe the latter.)

As a thank-you, I sent several signed paperback copies of my best-known novels to Stephen King, at his home address in Bangor, Maine. Inscribed on the title page of the most recent was the jest—

Not a stalker, Steve—
Just a fellow-writer!
With much admiration—

ANDREW J. RUSH

"Andy"
Mill Brook House
Harbourton, New Jersey

Of course I did not expect to receive a reply from such a busy person, and indeed I never did.

The parallels between Stephen King and Andrew J. Rush! Though I am sure they are only coincidental.

Not unlike Stephen King, who is said to have speculated that his extraordinary career might have been an accident of some kind, I have sometimes harbored doubts about my talent as a writer; I have felt guilt, that more talented individuals have had less luck than I've had, and might be justified in resenting me. About my devotion to my craft, my zeal and willingness to work, I have fewer doubts, for the simple truth is that *I love to write*, and am restless when I am not able to work at my desk at least ten hours a day. But sometimes when I wake, startled, in the night, for a moment not knowing where I am, or who is sleeping beside me, it seems to be utterly astonishing that I am a published writer at all—let alone the generally admired and well-to-do author of twenty-eight mystery-suspense novels.

These novels, published under my legal name, known to all— *Andrew J. Rush.*

There is another, curious similarity between Stephen King and me: as Stephen King experimented with a fictitious alter ego some years ago, namely *Richard Bachman,* so too I began to experiment with a fictitious alter ego in the late 1990s, when my career as *Andrew J. Rush* seemed to have stabilized, and did not require quite so much of my anxious energies as it had at the start. Thus, *Jack of Spades* was born, out of my restlessness with the success of *Andrew J. Rush.*

Initially, I'd thought that I might write one, possibly two novels as the cruder, more visceral, more frankly horrific "Jack of Spades"—but then, ideas for a third, a fourth, eventually a fifth pseudonym novel came to me, often at odd hours of the night. Waking, to discover that I am grinding my back teeth—or, rather, *my back teeth are grinding of their own accord*—and shortly thereafter, an idea for a new "Jack of Spades" novel comes to me, not unlike the way in which a message or an icon arrives on your computer screen out of nowhere.

While Andrew J. Rush has a Manhattan literary agent, a Manhattan publisher and editor, and a Hollywood agent, with whom he has long been associated, so too "Jack of Spades" has a (less distinguished) Manhattan literary agent, a (less distinguished) Manhattan publisher and editor, and a (virtually unknown) Hollywood agent, with whom he has been associated for a shorter period of time; but while "Andy Rush" is known to his literary associates, as to his neighbors and friends in Harbourton, New Jersey, no one has ever met "Jack of Spades" whose *noir* thrillers are transmitted electronically and whose contracts are negotiated in a similar impersonal fashion. Dust jacket photos of Andrew J. Rush show an affably smiling, crinkly-eyed man with a receding hairline against a background of book-crammed bookshelves, who more resembles a high school teacher than a bestselling mystery writer; no photos of "Jack of Spades" exist at all, it seems, and where you would expect to see an author photograph on the back cover of his books, there is startling (black) blankness.

Online, there are no photos of "Jack of Spades," only just reproductions of the writer's several (lurid, eye-catching) book covers, a scattering of reviews, and terse biographical speculation that makes me smile, it is so naïve, and persuasive—*"Jack of Spades" is said to be the pseudonym of a former convict who began his writing career while incarcerated in a maximum security prison in New Jersey on a charge of manslaughter. He is said to be currently on parole and working on a new novel.*

Alternatively, and equally persuasively, "Jack of Spades" has been identified as *a criminologist, a psychiatrist, a professor of forensic medicine, a (retired) homicide detective, a (retired) pathologist* who lives variously, in Montana, Maine, upstate New York and California as well as New Jersey.

"Jack of Spades" has also been identified, most irresponsibly, as a *habitual criminal, possibly a serial killer, who has committed countless crimes since boyhood without being apprehended, or even identified. Invariably, his true name, like his whereabouts, is "unknown."*

No one wants to think that "Jack of Spades" is *only a pseudonym,* indeed of a bestselling writer who is no criminal at all but a very responsible family man and civic-minded citizen. That is not romantic!

It has been increasingly difficult to keep such a complicated secret, especially in a hyper-vigilant era of electronic spying, but through four novels by "Jack of Spades" and negotiations for the fifth I have managed to maintain a distance between Andrew J. Rush and "Jack of Spades."

That's to say, my mainstream associates know nothing of my *noir*-self. And how distressed they would be, to learn that Andrew—"Andy"—Rush of all people has established a secret writerly identity without their knowledge! It's as if a happily married wife has discovered that her husband has been unfaithful to her for years—while never giving the slightest hint that he isn't entirely happy with their marriage.

Oh Andrew—how could you! This is so, so shocking . . .

In the early hours of the morning when I am wakened jolting from sleep, lying beside Irina who trusts me utterly, it is words like these that make my heart clench with guilt.

. . . and the novels of "Jack of Spades" . . . so shocking, depraved . . .

Yes, I have to concede: if I had not penned the *noir* novels of Jack of Spades myself, I would be repelled by them.

Of course, my/our identity has not (yet) been revealed. I am determined that it never will be.

It has been my fantasy that Jack of Spades would kill to retain his identity—though of course, Andrew J. Rush would never dream of harming anyone. (Perhaps this isn't entirely accurate: I have probably dreamt of "harming" some persons who deserve punishment. But I would never in waking life countenance any *punishment outside the criminal justice system* and when I am interviewed, I state that, given the vicissitudes of our criminal justice system in the United States, in which racism is rampant, I do not believe in capital punishment.) Of the two, it is Jack of Spades who thinks more highly of himself as a writer, or "visionary"; Andrew J. Rush has a more modest hope of being admired as an excellent writer of entertaining murder mysteries. Yet, Andrew Rush won an Edgar Award for best first mystery novel some years ago, and has been nominated for other awards, while Jack of Spades has never been singled out—so far—for any distinction.

Well, perhaps that is not entirely true. Online lists of *Best of Noir, Most Extreme Noir, X-Rated Noir,* etc., have often included titles by Jack of Spades, and it is fair to say that Jack of Spades has an underground, cultish following of a few thousand persons, at a modest estimate.

Why I feel such anxiety about my secret being revealed, I don't really know; it isn't as if I am a common criminal, after all! My IRS payments on the money accrued by "Rush" and "Jack of Spades," though complicated, involving not one but two accountants, are meticulously executed; I am not defrauding the U.S. government of a penny. (In one of his early novels Jack of Spades describes in lurid detail the evisceration of an IRS agent who has pried into the private life of a psychopath billionaire—but Andrew J. Rush is only repelled by such sensationalist prose.) Indeed, I love my quiet, blandly predictable suburban life, as a more or less conventional "family man"—I am a Brooks Brothers type, and often wear a necktie, for I like the feeling of snugness around my neck, as of a self-styled noose; it is "Bohemian" of me—(my family teases)—to wear Birkenstocks, and to go a few days without shaving so that I resemble, in a blurry mirror, one of those action film stars whose heavy jaws are covered in glinting quills, like atavistic predators. I have been a good, dutiful, if sometimes distracted son to my aging but still quite fit parents, who live in downtown Harbourton, in the red brick and stucco house on

Myrtle Street where I grew up, and who are touchingly proud of their "famous bestseller" son whose books they read with much pride and enjoyment; I have been a good, dutiful, if sometimes distracted husband to Irina, whom I'd met when we were undergraduates at Rutgers in the early 1980s; my three now-grown children would surely attest that I have been a very good, even "terrific" (their word) dad, with whom (probably) they have never felt entirely comfortable, for what writer is reliably *there* for his children, even when they require him? And what husband is continually, over the years, *there* for his wife, even when he adores her?

These are open secrets, so to speak. Of the kind we dare not articulate, for fear of wounding those close to us.

(As Jack of Spades has no one close to him, still less no one whom he adores, he wouldn't worry in the slightest about revealing any secrets!)

Though I am a very even-tempered individual now in my early fifties, I am sure that, as a boy, I was afflicted with a severe case of "ADD"—"Attention Deficit Disorder." When I was in grade school it was virtually impossible for me to sit still at a desk, and to keep from talking to, and occasionally pummeling, my classmates. Though teachers seemed to like me, overall, and to praise my schoolwork, I could not have been an easy child to have in a classroom for I felt at times as if red ants were inside my clothes, stinging and biting. I felt compelled to jump out of my seat, and scratch my body everywhere, and scream—such words I scarcely knew—curses, obscenities! (But I never did, of course. By the age of ten, I'd learned to—literally—bite my tongue, as well as the interior of my mouth; I learned to grind my back teeth, to force calmness upon me.) My parents scolded me when I "had the fidgets" (as they called it) but I do not believe that I was ever physically disciplined, or severely reprimanded.

Also, I was prone to accidents! Tripping and falling, scraping my knees, spraining an ankle, or a wrist; running too quickly downstairs, falling and cracking my head against a banister; near-drowning in the swimming quarry in Catamount State Park when I'd dived—(or been pushed by an older boy)—off the high board when I was twelve years old.

Often now, hearing the cries from a distance—*That boy! He's sinking! Save him . . .*

Just below the diving board. Looks like he struck his head . . .

With time I grew out of this chronic restlessness, which surely afflicts a percentage of children, especially young boys. Fortunately, the clinical diagnosis "ADD" didn't exist when I was a child, and restless children were not medicated, or I might have been narcotized at an early age, and my brain affected. (No one can tell me that dosing young children with such powerful drugs will have no long-term effect upon them.) And then again, in high school, from time to time I seemed to feel the urge to cut loose from my "good student" personality to join with pranksters and wise guys, though never more than temporarily—and secretly. For I did not want to jeopardize my mostly high grades and my upstanding reputation as *Most Reliable Boy* of the Class of '79.

It is annoying to me, but only just mildly—my Andrew J. Rush novels are not regularly reviewed in the *New York Times Book Review,* and then invariably in a roundup of mystery thrillers; and my "Jack of Spades" novels have not been reviewed once in the *Review,* no doubt because they are issued as paperback originals and, with their crude subject matter, and less than fussy writing, are perceived as beneath the radar of the *Times.* Yet, "Jack of Spades" sells surprisingly well for a virtually unknown and unadvertised writer: his first novel eventually sold about 35,000 copies, and continues to sell; his fourth, somewhere in the area of 50,000 to 60,000 copies, with the possibility of a film sale pending at the present time. (It will be all right with me if this sale doesn't go through, for publicity shone upon "Jack of Spades" might spill over onto Andrew J. Rush, which would be unfortunate. And I certainly don't need the money!) But just the other day an odd, unexpected item appeared in the "Arts" column of the *Times,* which I discovered purely by chance since no one who knows me would have drawn it to my attention:

Gryphon Books announces a new, fifth "Jack of Spades" title for their fall list, *Scourge.* It seems that "Jack of Spades" is not only a writer of decidedly *noir* mysteries but a Mystery Writer as well for no one seems to know who he, or she, is—including publisher, editor, and publicist at Gryphon. It is not even known where "Jack of Spades" lives—or if he/she is actually alive and not (as a rumor has suggested) the leftover manuscripts of a famous American misanthropic writer who allegedly died in 2006 of "suspicious causes."

I was stunned to read this—what nonsense! What irresponsible journalism! As groundless as even the rumors about "Jack of Spades" circulating online. Yet, for a panicked moment, I almost felt that there was in fact an individual known as "Jack of Spades" who was an independent, autonomous, quite unknown individual who was a stranger to *me*.

It had been relayed to the editorial staff at Gryphon Books that "Jack of Spades" was the pseudonym of a retired professional man living in the New York City area whose wish was to keep his writing career a secret even from his family; these minimal facts everyone at Gryphon had sworn to keep secret. And so when, via an e-mail account that could not easily be traced to me, in the guise of the agent who represented "Jack of Spades," I asked of the director of publicity at Gryphon Books who was saying the things about my client that had found their way into the *New York Times*, the young woman claimed that she had no idea. All she knew, she insisted, was what she'd been told—that is, told by the agent of "Jack of Spades." *He is a retired professional man living in the New York City area who insists on keeping his identity secret, and we will honor that wish.*

The thought came to me that I might have to terminate "Jack of Spades" after his fifth novel. For I would not want his connection to me—my connection to him—revealed. Such an erasure might be easily accomplished by simply ceasing to write under the pseudonym, without explanation to any agent or editor. Soon then, the *noir* writer would be forgotten, and his books out of print.

"Dad, what's this?"

My youngest child, Julia, visiting her mother and me for a weekend, happened to see a stack of paperbacks by "Jack of Spades" on a table in my study; the books with their *noir*-covers had been carelessly left in view, having been sent to me, from Gryphon, to a P.O. box in nearby Hadrian, New Jersey (which I rented for such clandestine "Jack of Spades" purposes). Usually when I bring "Jack of Spades" into this household it's to immediately hide the books away in a secure space in the basement adjacent to floor-to-ceiling shelves of translations of books by Andrew J. Rush at which no one ever glances. (After twenty-eight books, each of which has spawned numerous translations, you can imagine what an archive has collected in the shadowy basement!) My first-edition US and UK books are in built-in mahogany shelves in the living room, proudly displayed; it's against a background of such handsome, proper, hardcover books that "Andrew J. Rush" is customarily photographed.

"'Jack of Spades'—kind of a weird name! Of course, it's a pseudonym, I suppose."

To my horror there was my sweet-faced Julia leafing through *A Kiss Before Killing* with its lurid *noir* cover at which I could barely bring myself to glance. My heart was beating erratically, and a terrible heat (shame, guilt) suffused my face. What a blunder, to have left these paperbacks where anyone in the family could find them! My only solace was that there are always new books and galleys arriving in my study, as my family knows; and so these "Jack of Spades" paperbacks could easily be explained away as having been sent to me by a publisher requesting a blurb.

It was disconcerting, however, that Julia continued to glance through the book even as her face crinkled in distaste. Julia is the intellectual of our three children, having majored in linguistics and literary theory at Brown; a fascinating if useless major which hadn't seemed to help her find gainful employment, and so Julia had returned to school—to pursue a more useful graduate degree in sociology and social work at Rutgers-Newark. (Of course, Irina and I were underwriting this new academic adventure of Julia's, uncomplainingly. We had the money, after all!) Having been trained to "deconstruct" literature, rather than simply enjoy it, or react to it emotionally, Julia had honed her analytic and argumentative skills at Brown and had become, as a consequence, a sharp and relentless interrogator of her poor father "Andrew J. Rush" whose mystery-suspense novels, by the standards of literary theory, were hopelessly old-fashioned in plot, structure, language, and "vision"—the equivalent of, for instance, Dad's Brooks Brothers clothes, tame neckties, and Birkenstocks.

"Looks lurid but interesting. Obviously 'sexist'—old-style. Is 'Jack of Spades' anyone you know, Dad?"

No. Certainly he is not.

"Not one of your mystery-writer friends?"

No. Certainly he is not.

"What's his writing like?"

No idea. Haven't read.

"If you don't mind, Dad, maybe I'll borrow this 'Jack of Spades'—it's good for a feminist to know what the enemy is up to"—casually Julia set the paperbacks aside on the table.

By this time I'd broken into a sweat inside my clothes.

No no no no no. You will not.

Fortunately, Julia is an easily distracted young woman. I knew that, by the time she left us, mid-Sunday afternoon, she would have forgotten Jack of Spades entirely; and of course, clever Dad did not remind her.

By this time, in any case, I'd hidden the offensive paperbacks away in the secure space allotted to my alter ego, a storage room with a lock that had once been a fruit cellar in the farthest corner of the basement of our "historic" renovated house. If you happened to glance in that direction, which there is no reason for you to do, your gaze would be deflected by floor-to-ceiling metal shelves of Andrew J. Rush mysteries in translation, the more impressive for being indecipherable and impenetrable.

3   The Summons. June 2014.

"God *damn*."

If your name is *Rush,* to receive mail addressed to *Rash* is not flattering. Under other circumstances I would have tossed the envelope irritably aside.

But the address on the envelope was my own—Mill Brook House, 111 Mill Brook Road, Harbourton, New Jersey, and the return address was Hecate County Municipal Court, Harbourton, New Jersey—which prompted me to open it, with a pang of apprehension—(could this be a notice of a parking ticket? incurred in town unwittingly by me, or by Irina, using my car?). I saw that it wasn't a ticket, but it did seem to be a "summons"—rapidly skimming the thin green-tinted official document in which my name, doggedly misspelled as *Andwer J. Rash,* had been typed inexpertly.

Upon closer examination I saw that the summons was in fact a photocopy of an original court document complete with the seal of the State of New Jersey, but blurred and grainy as a partially remembered dream. I read the document through twice, with mounting impatience, and the second time my eye snagged on these startling words at the bottom of the page:

If Andwer J. Rash fails to appear in Hecate County Municipal Court on the date and at the time stated, a warrant will be issued for his arrest.

What was this? *Arrest?*

Several times I read these words without fully comprehending.

Standing very still, scarcely daring to breathe, the poorly photocopied document clutched in my fingers.

For here was a summons issued by the State of New Jersey, Hecate County Municipal Court on June 11, 2014, just three days previous, in compliance with a complaint issued against *Andwer J. Rash* by one *C. W. Haider* that the aforementioned had *committed an act of theft.*

"'Committed an act of—theft'?"

This was so preposterous, I laughed aloud.

Not an angry laugh, and not an amused laugh—a laugh of incredulity.

So far as I could determine from a close rereading of the smudged document an individual named "C. W. Haider" (of whom I had never heard) was accusing "Andwer J. Rash" of some sort of theft, the nature of which was undisclosed. The document was just a single-page form stating that "Owen S. Carson," a Harbourton Municipal Court judge, had signed the summons. On the next line, "Albert L. Steadman," Municipal

Court prosecutor, had signed his scrawling signature, and on the next, "Iris Flaherty," chief municipal clerk, had signed hers. The remainder of the document contained information about the Municipal Court with a particular focus on Traffic Court; there was no further reference to "Andwer J. Rash" and what he had been accused of doing in violation of any law.

To my horror I saw that the date for the hearing was just a few days from now: Monday morning at 9:00 A.M. in the courthouse on Chapel Street, Harbourton—the quaint limestone building, dating from 1741, a New Jersey State Landmark which Irina and I had helped to refurbish in a fund-raising campaign a few years ago.

The summons was tantamount to a subpoena, or an arrest warrant, it seemed—if "Andwer J. Rash" failed to appear in the quaint local court, he was subject to arrest.

The air about my head was gusty, though hot, and blindingly sunny—an unsettling combination.

In my emotional state, I scarcely knew where I was. A small child-voice protested—*But I have not stolen anything! I am innocent.*

I wasn't in my study but outdoors by the road in front of our house (though you could barely see our stone farmhouse from the road). As I often did at this hour of mid-afternoon I'd taken a break from work to hike out to the mailbox on our unpaved driveway; sometimes I jogged to the mailbox and back, and sometimes I rode my old English bike with its unfashionably narrow tires. Our driveway, which was nearly a quarter-mile long, led through the remains of an old pasture overgrown with meadow grasses and wildflowers and small trees. It was one of the beautiful walks of my life, that filled my eyes with tears, that somehow it had come to be *mine*.

Distractedly, I made my way back to the house. The other articles of mail—bills, magazines, flyers, a packet of fan mail forwarded by my publisher, even an envelope from my literary agency which probably contained a sizable check—meant so little to me, I would drop them in a heap on a table in the kitchen for Irina to discover later.

Inside the house, where the light wasn't so bright, and the air wasn't so agitated with the likelihood of a summer storm, I felt slightly calmer. Quickly I ascended the steps to my work-studio, shut the door and called the courthouse where after several rings the phone was answered as if reluctantly by the chief clerk Ms. Flaherty, in a voice as faint and begrudging as the poorly photocopied document. Trying to speak in an even tone I introduced myself and asked Ms. Flaherty to explain the summons; it took some time to identify it so that she could check her records; in so doing, Ms. Flaherty sighed often. Then, like a practiced bureaucrat, in a voice both chilly and defensive, she could tell me only that the summons issued by the court had to be "complied with"—I would have to appear in court on Monday morning, with or without "legal representation." At the hearing the charges would be explained and "evidence"—if there were any—would be introduced.

"'Evidence'—of what?"

The very term—*evidence*—was a sort of shock to me. For I must have been hoping that the chief clerk would tell me the summons had been a mistake, not meant for me at all.

Even now, I waited for the woman to laugh, and to apologize. For Ms. Flaherty seemed to be taking an undue amount of time to read the document which she herself had signed.

Stubbornly then she merely repeated what she'd already told me, that was of little help.

"'Evidence of theft'—but what am I accused of having stolen?"

My voice was raised in exasperation. Primly Ms. Flaherty said that such information would be given at the hearing, and that she had no idea what it might be.

"It's a serious charge—'theft.' I'm thinking that such a charge could be libelous."

When Ms. Flaherty did not reply I said that it was strange, if I'd been accused of theft, that a police officer had not come to my house to arrest me, with a warrant; and Ms. Flaherty said, "Mr. Rash, this is not criminal court—this is civil court. You would not be *arrested*."

Civil court! Of course. In my agitation I hadn't quite realized.

"But the warning is on the document—I am subject to arrest."

"Sir, that would be for 'contempt of court.' Not for a crime."

"But—if I am not guilty of a 'crime . . .'"

"Sir, that will be adjudicated. That is what the hearing is for."

With the fluency of a well-trained parrot Ms. Flaherty uttered the multi-syllabic *adjudicated*. As if expecting me to be daunted by this feat.

"Ms. Flaherty! Maybe you can't grasp the ludicrousness of this situation, but I can. At least tell me, please—who is 'C. W. Haiden'?"

"We don't give out such information, sir."

"But—this person, a stranger to me, is charging me with theft. What does this 'theft' entail?"

"I've told you, sir. That information isn't available. There's no one here in the office except me at the present time, and even if I wished to comply with your request, I could not."

Ms. Flaherty's voice was quavering with indignation. She seemed about to end our conversation. Urgently I asked if there was some way that I could find out what the charge was, to prepare for Monday, but she said, "Sir, I do not know. You may wish to retain counsel. That is what is usually done, in lawsuits."

"'*Lawsuits*'? I'm being sued?"

"I don't know, sir. That is what you will learn at the hearing."

"But you advise me to 'retain counsel'—even if I am wholly innocent, and have no idea what the hell is going on."

Audibly Ms. Flaherty drew in her breath. Was using the word *hell* tantamount to some sort of verbal harassment? Would I be charged with *sexual harassment*?

"Mr. Rash, there—"

"'Rush.' My name is 'Rush.'"

"Mr. Rush, there is—"

"You've consistently misspelled my name on this document. My name is 'Andrew J. Rush'—"

How pathetic it seemed to me, that I'd ever imagined that *Andrew J. Rush* was a "famous" name in Harbourton. The chief clerk of the Municipal Court had never heard of me, clearly.

"—and I can barely read this copy of the summons you sent me, the printing is so faint! This has got to be a mistake, and I don't want to be dragged to court on Monday for a mistake that isn't mine."

"Sir, court is in session at nine o'clock, Monday. Until then I can't give you any further information."

"But please, this is very upsetting—"

"Mr. Rash, I am going to hang up now. I would advise you to retain legal counsel, if you are concerned."

"'If I'm concerned'—is that a joke? Of course I'm concerned—I've been accused of theft, threatened with arrest, coerced into retaining a lawyer—"

"That is up to you, sir. No one is 'coercing' you."

"You must know, lawyers are God-damned expensive! Why should I pay a lawyer's exorbitant fee, if I am wholly innocent—if I don't even know what it is I've been accused of doing."

A rush of anger seemed to leap from me. As if, with his money, Andrew J. Rush couldn't afford a lawyer!

"Sir, good-bye."

"Wait! Ms. Flaherty, I need to know—"

But the line had gone dead. By this time my voice was raw and aggrieved.

I was thinking—*I am the one who will sue. This is outrageous.* Thinking—*But I have never stolen anything. Have I?*

Since the previous day, when my dear daughter Julia had innocently picked up a copy of Jack of Spades's *A Kiss Before Killing* and begun leafing through it, I had been feeling that something further would happen, out of my control. If there is one thing that frightens me, and infuriates me, it is losing control.

As if Jack of Spades had come to crouch in a corner of my life, unbidden by me, dragging all the light to him, and into him, like a black hole.

I could envision Irina overhearing me on the phone in another part of the house, startled and concerned. Though of the two of us Irina was the more emotional, the more easily upset, it sometimes happened that she heard me speaking intensely when I was alone in my study on the second floor of the house, over the garage—"Pleading, it sounds like"—when I am sure that I am not speaking at all, even on the phone; several times a week Irina will wake me out of a deep, turbulent sleep in the middle of the night, claiming that I'd been talking in my sleep, grinding my back teeth—"Calling for help."

At such times, so taken by surprise, it requires some seconds before I recognize Irina, my dear wife. More than once I've been concerned that, when Irina has shaken me to wake me from sleep, I've had an impulse to shove her away.

Already I was plotting how to keep this upsetting news from Irina, and from my family. I did not want to think that any "hearing" in the Harbourton Municipal Court must be publicly accessible, and might be reported in the *Harbourton Weekly*.

The phone rang. Eagerly I answered thinking it might be a repentant Ms. Flaherty, taking pity on me, calling back with helpful information, but instead it was Irina, on the downstairs extension, asking if something was wrong.

"Wrong? What could be wrong, darling? I've been having some difficulty with this new novel—that's all."

And it was so. I'd been having difficulty preventing my new mystery from continually metamorphosing into a more complicated, even imbricated structure than I'd planned, which I knew to be imprudent given the restrictions of the mystery genre. The title was *Criss-Cross* and its structure had been meant to be simple: a contrasting of "hero" and "villain" in alternating chapters until, in the final chapter, the "hero" prevails over the "villain." Readers of this genre have every right to expect that a contract of some implicit sort exists between them and the mystery authors—that "evil" will be punished sufficiently, and the usual chaos of the world will be radically simplified, to allow for an ending that is both plausible and unexpected.

Those intellectual-literary snobs who mock the restrictions of our genre—(including even dear Julia, whom I adore)—would find it very difficult to replicate a successful mystery themselves: one in which evil is pursued until it has been captured, and dealt with; and in which there is a clear and unambiguous *ending*.

The endings of Jack of Spades's mysteries were crueler, as they were more primitive. There was too much evil spilling over everything to be tidily mopped up and mostly, everybody died, or rather was killed. Often I had no idea how a novel by Jack of

Spades would end until the last chapter which came rushing at me like a speeding vehicle; mysteries by Andrew J. Rush were models of clarity carefully outlined months in advance, and rarely surprised the author.

This was good. For the author, as for my readers. No one likes surprises, essentially.

Irina was asking if I wanted her to come up to my study, if I was feeling anxious, and I thanked her but told her no, that wasn't necessary. There was only one cure for anxiety—work.

By dinnertime, I told her, I'd have worked myself out of the morass I was in. As I always did.

"If you're sure, Andrew . . . You know, you had another bad night last night."

I don't think so.

"Well—I seem to remember . . ."

Not at all, Irina. But thanks! Love you.

And I hung up, before the murmured echo *Love you.*

It was like my dear wife, I thought, to exaggerate. Irina had thought she'd overheard my uplifted voice just now, and she'd misinterpreted my mood. She seemed to have misremembered the previous night, which had been featureless as a dark, placid sea in which the turbulence of waves is indecipherable.

Such wifely solicitude is tender, when it is not exasperating!

In my fingers was a glass of wine—(tart white wine, my favorite)—which I hadn't remembered pouring.

4   The Accusation

"God *damn*."

Of course, I could not work! My heart was beating rapidly and my breathing felt constrained as if something, or someone, were tightening a hand around my chest.

Impulsively then, though I should have known better, I decided to call C. W. Haider. Any lawyer would have advised me not to try to communicate with this individual who'd accused me—(fraudulently, crazily)—of theft; but of course, I could not resist trying to appeal to his sense of justice and fair play. I could not resist thinking, with childish vanity—*But he will like me, when he hears my voice. Everyone likes Andy Rush!*

There appeared to be no "C. W. Haider" listed in the Harbourton directory but there were several Haiders living in town, on older, historic streets near the town square. No one answered the first two calls, but the third was answered on the second ring, by an individual with a bright expectant voice who might have been a precocious child, or a mildly retarded adult—"Yes-ss? Hel-lo?"

I asked if I might speak to "C. W. Haider" and the voice responded brightly, "You are! You are speaking to 'C. W. Haider.'"

A child! Or, a woman posing as a child.

Awkwardly I introduced myself. As I uttered "Andrew J. Rush" it seemed to me that I could hear an intake of breath at the other end of the line.

"I'm calling to inquire about a summons I received today from the Harbourton Municipal Court. 'C. W. Haider'—which you say is you—has filed a complaint with the court accusing me of theft. But I don't understand what the 'theft' could be, Ms. Haider. (It is 'Ms. Haider'—isn't it?) Are you actually claiming that I took something from you, when you must know we've never met?"

Silence. Again, a sound of breathing, close against the phone receiver.

"Hello? Is this—Ms. Haider? Are you there?"

Now the voice came in a low childish sly drawl—"Yes-ss."

"You've charged me with theft, you've issued a complaint with the municipal court, will you please explain *why*? What is it I'm supposed to have stolen from you?"

"*You* know."

"I know—what?"

"*You know what you took,* Mr. Rush."

The voice was louder now, sharper and not so childish.

"No. I don't. I don't know 'what I took'—I don't know who the hell 'C. W. Haider' is, or anything about you. I think you owe me the courtesy of an explanation, at least."

"Well, it has to stop. It has gone on too long, and now I am putting a stop to it. The judge will help me put a stop to it."

The voice lifted in shrill protest. You could imagine the eyes shining with indignation and hurt.

"A stop to what?"

"You know, Mr. Rush. You know what you are doing to me."

"But what is it that I'm doing?"

"Stealing from me. The pages you took, for your novels. The things that are mine, that you took. You are a plagi-a-rist—a *plagiarist*. I will expose you to the world."

"'Stealing'—'plagiarist'—you're accusing me of *plagiarism*? That's outrageous."

"It is outrageous! It is! That is why you will be exposed, and punished! *I want the things you have stolen returned, and I want you to apologize. And you owe me money—royalties.*"

"Is this a joke? Are you someone I know?"

"Yes! I am someone you know—*I am someone you have been stealing from.*"

"But—how is this possible? Stealing what? How?"

"Out of my house. You have been stealing out of my house, and it has to stop, and it will stop."

"But—this isn't true! I don't know you, or where you live—I don't have any idea what you are talking about. 'Pages'—'novels' . . ."

"The judge will punish you, on Monday! You will see, then. All of the world will see, then. Thief! Plagi-a-rist! They will vilify *you*."

33

The woman gave a wild little cry, a burst of childish laughter. The line went dead.

She is mad. Madness.
Nothing to do with you.
Call a lawyer. Do not become involved.

Dazed, disbelieving. For a long time I stood at an octagonal window in my study, staring into the distance—(the grassy meadow, a fleeting view of Mill Brook on the farther side of the road)—without seeming to see anything. My thoughts beat like great deranged wings. *Vilify,* she'd said. The word stung. *They will vilify you.*

Plagi-a-rist. A worse word.

Just kill her. Silence the voice, the threat will go away.
Through the millennia, that has been the most effective strategy.

Jack of Spades would not hesitate. Jack of Spades had a ready solution for any problem.

5   The Good Citizen

"It has to be a misunderstanding. Why would she select *me*."

With a part of my mind I understood that "C. W. Haider" was mentally ill, and that this bizarre accusation had nothing to do with "Andrew J. Rush" personally; yet with another part of my mind I felt threatened as if physically under siege.

I had never been accused of any crime before, nor even any misdemeanor. Through my life of more than five decades, I'd accumulated, perhaps, less than a half-dozen parking and speeding tickets.

I had never been sued. I had never been "arrested."

I had never been served a summons. A subpoena.

Wanting to protest to C. W. Haider: I am a good person! I am a person who loves his family, and I am a citizen who cares about his community.

I am a person whom others respect, admire, love.

I am not a petty criminal.

I am not a plagiarist!

You will not vilify me!

It was in 1998 that Irina and I made the decision to buy Mill Brook House, as it's called. A somewhat overgrown, just-slightly-shabby but beautiful eleven-acre property north of the village of Harbourton within view of meandering Mill Brook.

We bought the property, or rather made a down payment and acquired a mortgage, with money from the sales of my first several novels. We were not rich—hardly!—but suddenly, it seemed that we had money, we could afford to live on a scale we'd never have anticipated when I began writing and sending out my work with the blind optimism of a man fishing with a half-dozen lines.

Until then we'd been living in a small ranch-style house in suburban New Brunswick where I taught English at Highland Park High School, and Irina was a Montessori instructor. *Humdrum* is the word that comes to mind—though I try to beat it away as you'd beat away a loud-buzzing fly it is *humdrum* that comes to mind most ignominiously.

Humdrum lives for humdrum folks.

Before Jack of Spades emerged out of Nowhere.

Often we visited my parents in Harbourton forty miles to the west and south, where I'd been born and grown up and still had—still have—many friends from childhood. *Humdrum life too* it had been there—probably—but my memories are happy ones, overall. My father was a small-town merchant (footwear, ladies' handbags) who did moderately well in the context of other Harbourton merchants and who never complained of his life though when I was a boy of about thirteen, seeing Dad's store on Main Street, one glass-fronted facade among others, each showcasing merchandise to the street, a dizzying realization came to me: *What if no one buys? Suddenly—from now on—no one?*

There is terror in such a realization, when you are thirteen.

It is not the terror of split skulls, spilled blood, death. It is the *humdrum terror* of ordinary life.

Did I say that I had a happy childhood? In interviews, this is so.

It is often the case that an *only child* has a happy childhood because there are no rivals for his parents' love.

North of Harbourton is rolling farmland, beautiful countryside bordering Mill Brook and long the property of wealthy landowners, multi-millionaire retired businessmen and politicians. For those of us who grew up in Harbourton it was a romantic dream to someday buy one of the old country estates along Mill Brook.

But—can we afford it? Irina asked.

We can afford it, darling! I promise you.

We spent more than a year renovating the eighteenth-century farmhouse with its small rooms, slanted plank floors, and unnervingly steep, narrow staircases. The original cellar was earthen-floored, with an oppressive, low ceiling; many of the windows were ill-fitting, and the house was prohibitively expensive to heat. We added rooms, we built a guest wing. In a room adjacent to the living room, with floor-to-ceiling bookshelves, I began to collect favorite books of mine in their earliest editions, when I could find them: American mystery and detective fiction of the

1930s, 1940s, 1950s; a miscellany of pulp magazines containing "weird tales" of H. P. Lovecraft; first or early editions of books by Edgar Allan Poe, Ambrose Bierce, Algernon Blackwood, M. R. James, Robert W. Chambers, Richard Matheson; ghost stories by Henry James and Edith Wharton; science fiction of a philosophical nature by Isaac Asimov, Philip K. Dick, J. G. Ballard; a solid wall of mid- and late-twentieth-century contemporaries from *A* to *Z,* through Barker, King, Le Guin, Morrow, Straub . . .

My writing room, which has been featured in the *New York Times Style Magazine* as well as in *New Jersey Life,* is on the second floor of the farmhouse, in an extension built over the garage (formerly a stable). This light-filled room has skylights and windows overlooking a grassy decline to a large pond on which waterfowl—(mallards, Canada geese, swans)—languidly paddle. Beyond is a deciduous forest, which is part of our property; beyond that, just visible from my study, the gray-blue curve of Mill Brook. At a draftsman's table in this room I compose my novels on a computer, working with hand-scrawled notes; on the wall beside the table I affix maps, plot outlines, hand-drawn likenesses of my "characters," chronological lists. For I am a meticulous plotter of mysteries—even those readers who dislike my novels for their inevitable upbeat endings have to concede that no one plots mystery novels more conscientiously than Andrew Rush.

On a windowsill facing the draftsman's table are my magical talismans—family pictures, my Edgar first novel award, mementos and good-luck charms.

In a small refrigerator, quick-energy supplies: orange juice, almond-yogurt bar, Diet Coke, white wine.

I am so happy here.

Here is my soul.

You will not dare separate me from my soul.

On the farther side of the room facing a smaller window is a smaller table, reputedly an antique, curiously scarred as if with a penknife, bought from a local Mill Brook Valley dealer. It is on this table that I compose my "Jack of Spades" novels first by hand, on yellow legal paper; then, when I have accumulated several chapters, I bring the material to the draftsman's table to type into the computer.

File. *J.S.*

Writing as "Jack of Spades," I write very quickly, and rarely glance back. Unlike "Andrew J. Rush," I don't plot carefully at all—I scarcely think in terms of *plot*.

One thing happens, and then another.

And another.

And then—there's a (nasty) surprise.

Writing as "Jack of Spades" I rarely write before midnight. When the rest of the house is darkened. When I am totally alone, and not likely to be interrupted. When the tartest of white wines won't do the trick and a few ounces of Scotch whiskey tastes very good—*very* good.

"Jack of Spades" is my reward for having written a minimum of ten to twelve pages on my own novel—that's to say, the novel that will next appear under the name "Andrew J. Rush."

If I postpone writing as "Jack of Spades" until the early hours of the morning, I can assume that my energy won't flag as it inevitably flags writing as "Andrew J. Rush."

Wild ride. Roller coaster.

And suddenly—the tracks have vanished in midair.

Sometimes I find myself back in Catamount Park. Where when you were a kid you hid your fear of the roller coaster and the high diving board at the quarry. And other things.

Catamount Park is a state park in Far Ridge, about an hour's drive from Myrtle Street, Harbourton, where we lived at the time.

When we were boys. Brothers.

At the quarry, climbing the clay-colored misshapen boulders to the rocky promontory above the water. There, the high diving board.

There were two diving boards at the quarry: the higher, the lower. The more daring, the less daring. One for older boys, one for younger boys. Children, girls, most adults swam in the "safe" part of the quarry. Teenaged boys, guys in their twenties and older guys who were practiced swimmers and show-off divers clambered over the boulders to get to the rocky promontory that was the highest point.

Younger boys were not always welcome. Depending upon who was there, and what time of day.

And in the near distance, tinkly music from the merry-go-round. Cries and laughter from the roller coaster.

Some of us (boys) were obsessed with the (higher) diving board.

"Andrew? Is something wrong?"

It was Irina, behind me.

I did not turn—not at once. Though I had not heard Irina approach me the hairs on the nape of my neck had begun to stir in apprehension.

"I thought I heard someone talking. Unless it was a TV turned up high."

No TV. Not here.

My dear wife had wakened at 2:35 A.M. and saw that I hadn't come to bed and so went to look for me and found me in my study in a far wing of the house seated at the scarred antique desk with a single lamp burning, wholly absorbed in writing—writing rapidly, by hand, on the legal pad.

Trying to remain calm, calmly smiling, yes and smiling with my eyes as well as my mouth—"Irina! Why aren't you asleep, darling?"

"I was asleep, Andrew. I went to bed at eleven. But—I've been missing you."

Irina came forward, hesitantly. She was in a silky beige night-gown, and barefoot. Her body seemed attenuated, flattened. The soft slack small breasts, the just discernibly protuberant stomach. Her short, dark-blond, graying hair was matted on one side of her head. In the wan light her face appeared pale and insubstantial as a paper mask, faintly lined. Beneath her concerned eyes, shadows like smudges.

Wife, mother, helpmeet. It is good of you to love her.

But why do you love her? Is she not one of those who have worn out your love?

A wife is an emotional parasite. You are the parasite's host.

Easily, the wife's skull might be broken in a fall.

In the night, on the steep steps—easily.

Quickly I laid down my pen, and pushed away the yellow legal pad so that, if Irina came to me, she could not glance down—(as if innocently)—and see what I'd been writing.

Irina respects my need for privacy, when I am writing; it is rare for her to enter my writing room uninvited.

So too, when they were growing up, the children respected Daddy's need for privacy. Though it was rare to punish them, only rather to discipline them.

Ridiculous, to be playing "Daddy"!

Too many years of playing Daddy!

No more Daddy than Jack of Spades is Daddy.

"Well. I didn't mean to interrupt you, Andrew. Come to bed when you can."

Irina spoke uncertainly. She must have wanted to come to me, to touch my shoulder, the back of my neck—a wifely gesture. Was there something in my face that discouraged her?

A woman is particularly desirable when she feels, or imagines that she feels, subtly rebuked. In that instant of turning away, glimpsed in profile, when you might still call her back . . .

"Irina, darling—wait!"

I pushed away from the little table—I hurried after my dear wife of nearly a quarter-century. My heart beat quickly with desire and hope and a wish to hold the woman tightly and to be held by her tightly.

The hell with "Jack of Spades"—that night.

Entering my study in the morning I perceived that something had been altered. Almost I'd thought that an intruder had been here!

At first I could not make out what was wrong or out of place, then I saw that the lamp on the smaller worktable lay on its side, as if it had been pushed over; the lightbulb had shattered. When I checked the switch, the light was still *on.*

A six-ounce (empty) glass smelling of whiskey had left a faint ring on the antique wood of the table.

A dozen or more pages of yellow legal paper were covered in an indecipherable scrawl barely recognizable as my own and the pen with which I'd been writing had fallen to the floor and lay several feet away as if it had been flung down in fury.

"How does it feel to be a 'local celebrity'? The 'most famous writer' in Hecate County? One of the 'bestselling' writers in New Jersey?"—so I have been asked by well-intentioned interviewers, who seem not to notice that such questions are deeply embarrassing to any writer of integrity.

Quickly and quietly I aver that I am very grateful for the "modest success" I've had, and try to change the subject.

However, it is true that my writing "success" has changed the lives of myself and my family considerably. I have hoped to express my gratitude by being generous to others less fortunate.

For instance, I have endowed one of those "emergency" funds for writers administered by the Writers Guild. I have endowed scholarships at Harbourton High where I'd graduated in the Class of '79. Irina and I have made contributions to the local animal shelter and we've helped build a new wing of the Harbourton Public Library which has a permanent exhibit titled BESTSELLING MYSTERIES BY HECATE COUNTY'S OWN ANDREW J. RUSH. (Embarrassing! But I don't interfere in the operations of the library.) We've given annually to literacy programs in such beleaguered New Jersey cities as Newark, Trenton, and Camden and we've participated in NJN-TV (New Jersey Network) literacy fund-raisers. We've helped refurbish the funky old Cinema Arts Theatre on South Main where, on occasional Friday evenings, Andy Rush acts as an amateur M.C. introducing classic mystery and *noir* films like *Shadow of a Doubt, Vertigo, Diabolique, Niagara, The Shining, The Vanishing.* We've given money for the new softball field and to the Harbourton Little League in which I'd once played (not badly) as a boy. (Indeed, it is embarrassing to acknowledge that the new softball field is named after me—*Andrew J. Rush Field.*) Now that the children are grown and gone from us Irina has returned to work (part-time) at the progressive Friends School in nearby Hadrian where she teaches art and where she is active in the PTA. Irina Rush has been a tutor in the New Jersey Literacy Program for several years.

In 2010, I received a Citizen's Award from the New Jersey Association for Responsible Citizenship. Just last year, I received a Governor's Medal from the State of New Jersey for my philanthropic contributions. And next year, it has been promised— (that is, there is a rumor to this effect)—that I will be honored by induction into the New Jersey Hall of Fame as one of the state's "most cherished" contributors to the arts.

And my most acclaimed works of fiction lie before me. I am sure.

God damn you I am not a thief, and I am not a plagiarist and I am not to be vilified by anyone.

6   "We Will Bury Her"

"It's a nuisance suit, Andrew. The judge will toss it out. We'll demand legal costs, and an injunction to block such 'harassment of the artist' in the future."

He spoke with such lawyerly confidence, and such solicitude for me, I felt a wave of relief but also the faint incredulity of one who has expected to hear a death sentence and has heard instead that he has been reprieved.

In the morning I'd done what I should have done as soon as I'd received the summons from the Harbourton court the previous day: I called my editor in New York City who referred me to the legal department at my publishing house and within minutes I was being reassured by a lawyer named Elliot Grossman that there was nothing to worry about, absolutely—"Don't give this ridiculous 'complaint' a second thought. It won't go any further, I predict. Andrew? Are you listening?"

Am I listening? I was gripping the phone receiver so tightly, my fingers ached.

"Yes, I—I've heard, Elliot. Thank you . . ."

My voice trailed off in wonderment. Was the summons such a trivial matter, were my fears totally unfounded? "C. W. Haider" wasn't a threat to my reputation? My career? My *life*?

On the phone, Elliot Grossman sounded like an eminently reasonable man. We had never met at the publishing house—we had never had any reason to confer together before this on any matter. He'd asked me to fax the summons to him and after he'd read it carefully he called me back to allay my fears. He seemed to understand that I was one of those persons who, however they know themselves to be "innocent" of any crime, are thrown into a state of anxiety at the mere possibility of a lawsuit.

"I'll be happy to take the case, Andrew. Of course! I'm a great admirer of your novels."

To this, I murmured a vague *Thank you.*

Whether Elliot Grossman was sincere or otherwise, it was a courteous thing for him to say. Especially to a writer as uncertain of his worth as Andrew Rush.

"I'll be in Harbourton on Monday morning for the hearing, promptly at nine A.M., Andrew. But I'll go alone, you needn't attend. As long as you are 'represented' there is no reason for you to attend, and I advise you not to."

"Really? I thought the summons stipulated . . ."

"No. This is just a hearing, not a trial. The judge will be impressed that anyone shows up at all for such a frivolous suit. I seriously doubt that any 'warrant' would have been made out for your arrest—that's ridiculous. The judge will be flattered that a publishing house as distinguished as ours is sending 'legal counsel'—he'll dismiss within five minutes. Complaints like these are not uncommon, and frivolous lawsuits against purportedly famous or wealthy persons are not uncommon. It's a form of blackmail with which the law is well acquainted, and the Harbourton judge will recognize it for what it is. Given the nature of the complainant, as you've described her to me, I'd guess that she might be already known to the court—a classic crank."

Grossman spoke zestfully in the way of one whose profession is such speech: staccato bursts of words, and a pleasure in words that was virtually kinetic.

"I've represented a number of writers, over the years, who've been sued for 'theft'—'plagiarism' more often 'libel' and 'invasion of privacy.' With our First Amendment it's damned hard to make a case even when there *is a case*—which there isn't here, I'm sure."

I'm sure. This did not sound vehement enough to me.

"Andrew, you say you don't know this 'C. W. Haider'—yes? You've never visited her home, you've never read anything she has written?"

"Certainly not!"

"Well, sometimes strangers send writers manuscripts, and it's not advised to read these manuscripts but, if you can, return them immediately to the sender with a notification, signed and dated, that you have not read them. If you keep a manuscript, that might indicate that you've read it; and the writer might peruse whatever you write afterward, to see if you've 'plagiarized' from him—or her. It isn't uncommon, Andrew. You're lucky to have been spared until now."

Desperately I was trying to think: had I ever received anything from "C. W. Haider"? I was too embarrassed to tell Grossman that over the years I had occasionally read manuscripts sent to me by strangers, and, naïvely, I'd even written back to some of them with suggestions for revisions; in most cases, the writers expressed gratitude, though next they usually wanted an introduction to an agent or an editor, which took the correspondence to another level entirely—not always happily.

I told Grossman that I was almost certain, I'd never received any manuscripts or letters from "C. W. Haider" nor had I written to her; and Grossman said, with a chuckle, "If you have, Andrew, we will soon find out. She'll have the letters with her."

He went on to tell me that, of the writers he'd represented over the course of a twenty-year career, it was Stephen King who, not surprisingly, was the most frequent target of crank lawsuits; but that King had managed to avoid really serious litigation so far since the cases were usually demonstrably ridiculous.

"You've represented Stephen King?"—this was encouraging to me.

"Of course. More than once."

"Was he—upset at being sued?"

"Initially. But Steve got used to it, as a 'public figure'—it's like wearing a large target on your back. The flip side of fame, drawing the attention of the mentally unstable. And the litigious, who are a separate category, though they can also be mentally unstable."

"Were you always successful in defending Stephen King?"

Though it was not like me to be so rudely inquisitive I had to ask this question. Grossman laughed, obscurely.

"Well, Andrew—I think, in fairness to Steve, I shouldn't discuss his legal problems any further. Some of these cases are in the public record and you could look them up—others were settled out of court, and privately. And when Steve changed publishers, a few years ago, naturally I no longer represented him. I have no idea what has happened, if anything, in subsequent years. I just wanted you to know, to assuage your anxiety, because you've been sounding very anxious on the phone—I wanted you to know that you are not alone. Bestselling writers have always been targets for litigation."

"'Settled out of court, privately'—does that mean that Stephen King had to *pay*? Why on earth would he have to *pay*?"

"Andrew, please. It isn't uncommon for a well-to-do client to settle with an aggressive plaintiff, just to clear the air and avoid ugly publicity. A settlement doesn't have to be millions of dollars, as you might think from the media; I've managed settlements for as little as ten thousand, one notable time just *nine hundred ninety-nine dollars*."

"But if the writer is 'innocent'—"

"Of course! Of course the writer is 'innocent'! Writers of the stature of Stephen King and Andrew J. Rush are hardly likely to 'plagiarize' their material from amateurs and lunatics."

Stammering I told Grossman that I thought, in this case, that the complainant was actually accusing me of breaking into her house and taking something . . .

But a seasick sensation had come over me. I could not have said with any clarity what I did think and I could not have brought myself to re-examine the summons which by this time I'd read, reread and reread to the point of nausea.

Grossman laughed. "Andrew, that's wild! As long as it doesn't get into the media, it's really funny—you must admit. 'Breaking and entering'—crawling through a window—to steal ideas for your novels from 'C. W. Haider.'"

I did not think this was funny. I did not laugh.

As long as it doesn't get into the media.

Better to erase the accuser at once.

In his exuberant way, no longer so reassuring to me as it had been, Grossman spoke for another half hour outlining his strategy for the hearing on Monday, which involved some emergency detective work, and reiterating his advice that I stay away. "The plaintiff will see you and no doubt recognize you and this will be exciting to her. If she's mentally unbalanced as we think she is, it could provoke an ugly scene. It's exactly what stalkers want—forcing a confrontation with the rich and famous."

Stalker? Rich and famous? Grossman's words swarmed about me like buzzing gnats. I was trying to feel a small dim stir of pride at being called, however extravagantly, *rich and famous;* I was trying not to feel panic at hearing *stalker.*

So far as I knew, so far as the summons indicated, and our brief phone conversation suggested, C. W. Haider wasn't (yet) "stalking" me.

The woman lived on Tumbrel Place, however, not far from the courthouse and municipal buildings. By my estimate, less than five miles from Mill Brook House.

This was a new fear, which Grossman had unwittingly put into my mind—*stalker.*

Better to make the preemptive strike, friend.

Better to kill at once.

As if he'd just thought of it Grossman asked if I had ever spoken with "C. W. Haider"—on the phone, for instance?

Now the seasick sensation deepened. For of course I should not have called the person whose name was on the summons as a complainant—I'd known better, and yet I had called her. Shame-faced now I told Grossman that yes, unfortunately I had called the woman yesterday afternoon, soon after receiving the summons. "I'd just wanted to know what the charge actually was—what I've been accused of stealing. The conversation did not go well."

For a stunned moment, Grossman was quiet. That so verbal a man was without words was not a good sign.

"The woman did sound unbalanced—it was hard to understand her. She has a strange, high, wild laugh . . ."

My voice trailed off, weakly. I felt like a child who has not only disobeyed an elder, but stupidly disobeyed.

"Well. This is unfortunate, Andrew. You should never have tried to contact the plaintiff, of course. I would have thought that someone of your intelligence and experience . . ." Grossman paused, pointedly. I did not want to imagine the expression on his face.

Guiltily I tried to explain: "I'd meant only to ask a few questions. It was a short exchange. I spoke very courteously. She said that I'd taken things 'out of her house'—and that it 'had to stop . . .'"

"You didn't threaten *her*, I hope?"

"Of course not. I would not ever threaten anyone."

"We can pretend this didn't happen. That might be for the best. If there were a trial—(which I'm sure there will not be, please don't panic)—the phone record would be put into evidence, and you couldn't deny it. But this isn't a trial, and no one is sworn in. And you won't even be there. So let's just hope for the best. Maybe she won't mention a call."

Still I blundered, shamefaced. Badly I wanted to regain Elliot Grossman's regard for me. "The worst of it was, I'd known beforehand that I shouldn't have called her. But I guess I hoped that she would listen to reason. That she would see that I'm a nice person . . ."

I could not bring myself to tell him—*I wanted to avoid calling a lawyer. I am afraid of lawyers.*

"Andrew, you should know that your legal adversary does not want to perceive you as a *nice person* and there is nothing you can do to convince her that you are not her enemy but a *nice person*. It wasn't a smart move to contact her, my friend, but at least you told me. I'm grateful for that. As long as you didn't threaten her, or try to cajole her into withdrawing the complaint, and she hasn't recorded the conversation—I think we will be fine."

Grossman's voice had shifted its tone. He was businesslike, brusque.

"I'll call you immediately after the hearing, Andrew—no need to call me. Just put this out of your mind entirely. I assure you—nothing will come of 'C. W. Haider.' *We will bury her.*"

7   A Kiss Before Killing

"Andy, Julia is upset about something."

Irina spoke hesitantly. By her tone I understood that our youngest daughter's distress had something to do with me and that Irina was being cautious in bringing the subject up to me as if—absurdly, and unfairly—she feared my reaction.

It is very annoying to me when members of my own family approach me with caution. It is utterly baffling.

"What? What is Julia upset about?"

"A novel she read by someone who calls himself 'Jack of Diamonds'—I think that's the name. She says she thinks that this writer is someone who knows you, a mystery-writer friend of yours, and she thinks that the writer, whoever he is, used something that had happened to *her* in his novel."

"Wait, Irina. I don't follow this. What are you saying?"

It was the eve of the hearing. Sunday night, and less than twelve hours until nine o'clock Monday morning in the Hecate Municipal Courthouse.

I had not told Irina, of course. My dear wife must be spared emotional upsets.

My heart beat hard. Guilt, guilt.

It is very hard to be a parent of integrity.

"Julia will tell you herself, Andy. But she called me first, and she was crying. This awful 'Jack of Diamonds'—"

"Who? What?"

"—a mystery writer who calls himself 'Jack of Diamonds'— or maybe it's 'Jack of Hearts'—some sort of hard-boiled crime writer, definitely a misogynist, and a brute, like Mickey Spillane . . ."

As if Irina had ever read a novel by Mickey Spillane!

In my collection of first edition American mystery fiction there were a number of Spillane titles from the 1950s, purchased in secondhand bookstores; but no one in my family had touched these since we'd moved into Mill House and reshelved the books, I was sure.

"Julia says there's a scene in this 'Jack of Hearts' novel she just read that replicates almost exactly the time when she fell through that rotted pedestrian bridge in Battlefield Park, and might have been killed—except in the novel, the child *was killed.*"

This was a melancholy memory! I would rather not have been reminded.

Julia had been four years old. A lively, inquisitive little girl. We were living in Highland Park at this time, adjacent to New Brunswick; one day I took Julia to Battlefield Park a few miles away, and there (to my shame) I'd become distracted by taking notes, working on a scene in one of my novels, and Julia wandered off beside a creek following some quacking geese and without my noticing she climbed up onto a pedestrian bridge that was no longer in use; such a little girl, she had no trouble crawling through the blockade, laughing at how clever she was to slip away from Daddy though Daddy had told her not to wander off—Daddy had certainly warned her *not to wander off*. And suddenly then Julia's little foot plunged through the rotted wood of the bridge. She screamed as part of the bridge collapsed, and she fell about twelve feet into the creek bed, her fall miraculously interrupted by underbrush so that she was unhurt except for scratches, bruises, and the trauma of the fall.

"Julia says there's a scene in this novel that is almost exactly like her accident, it's even set in a place called 'Battle Park'—not in New Jersey but upstate New York."

"A coincidence . . ."

My voice was faint, quavering.

Battle Park! How stupidly renamed, when the original had been Battlefield Park.

"I told Julia, of course it's just a coincidence. But it is strange and upsetting, isn't it?"

"I suppose it would be, if Julia takes it so personally. Is the little girl in the novel anything like her?"

A strange question! Fortunately, Irina didn't seem to notice.

"Julia said that, in the novel, the little girl dies—her skull is broken in the fall. The father who has taken her into the park is an evil man who is in fact the little girl's stepfather, not her father. He resents his wife's children and plots to kill them, through 'accidents.'"

Vaguely I recalled the plot of *A Kiss Before Killing*. It was characteristic of the pseudonymous novels that, rapidly written as they were, in a kind of white-heat of inspiration in the early hours of the morning, I could not remember them in much detail even by the time they were published, let alone a few years later.

"Julia said that the plot of the novel was very clever—but repulsive. The evil stepfather is never suspected of arranging any of the 'accidents'—he is always stricken with guilt, it seems genuinely, and feels remorse; until another 'accident' happens to another child. Julia said she couldn't continue reading the novel any further, to see how it ended."

"Well, good! Just throw 'Jack of Spades' out."

"'Jack of Spades'? Is that the name of the—writer?"

Irina blinked at me as if a bright blinding light were shining in her face. Though I love my dear wife very much there are moments when Irina's very sweetness—the *simplicity of her sweetness*—is deeply annoying.

"Yes, darling. You've been talking about 'Jack of Spades' for the past ten minutes—how Julia has been upset by a novel of his."

"Yes. Julia is upset. And I am upset, to think that a private, very personal incident in our lives has been exploited by a stranger . . . If that is what happened."

"Well, darling—that's a big 'if'! I doubt we could sue 'Jack of Spades' for invasion of privacy on such slender evidence."

"No one wants to sue anyone. But . . ."

I was feeling edgy, impatient. I wanted to protest to Irina that I was in no way responsible for this latest crisis of Julia's.

Since they became teenagers, and now that they are adults, there are too often crises of some kind in our children's lives. A call home, a conversation with Irina, the latest debacle, the latest disappointment or reversal of fortune or betrayal, a need for emotional support, *a need for money*—all too familiar.

Though I am the quintessential American father—dear old Dad with open arms, dimpled smile, checkbook.

Dimply-smiling Dad. Asshole.

Hadn't I warned Julia not to read Jack of Spades? Hadn't I hidden the damned books away? Obviously, Julia had disobeyed me—as she, and her older brothers, had so often disobeyed their clueless Daddy when they'd lived in this house.

I wanted to protest to Irina that I was not a friend of Jack of Spades and even if I were, I'd never have spoken to him about our little daughter's near-fatal accident in Catamount Park. And in any case Julia hadn't died—had she?

How strange I was feeling! Perspiration on my face, beneath my arms, inside my clothes. Between my fingers a glass of wine—tart white wine, from a local New Jersey winery whose owner is a "great admirer" of Andrew J. Rush—which I didn't remember pouring.

Or maybe, Irina had brought me the glass of wine. To placate me, to make me less anxious.

I was remembering now: not Catamount Park, but Battlefield Park.

And Julia hadn't died. Had not.

Irina was telling me that Julia would be joining us for dinner that evening, but was really coming over to speak with me about *A Kiss Before Killing*. Irina didn't plan to be part of the conversation—"It's between you and her. You know how emotional Julia can be, and how she depends upon your advice. I hope you'll be patient with her, Andrew."

This too was annoying. Subtly insulting for my wife to suggest that I am less patient with the children than she is.

"Daddy, it can't be just a coincidence! I don't believe that."

Julia looked at me with an expression of childish hurt and exasperation. As if somehow, but how would Julia *know how,* Daddy was to blame.

It seemed that, though Julia had forgotten to take the Jack of Spades novel with her last week, she'd remembered the unusual pseudonym and picked up *A Kiss Before Killing* on her own.

Plaintively she was saying: "In the novel, the little girl dies when she falls and cracks her skull on the rocks in the creek bed. The stepfather is sorry—sort of—though he'd been imagining that she might fall. Then, later, there's another 'accident' involving her brother—and her brother dies. I stopped reading at that point."

Smiling, I tried to console my daughter. Since childhood Julia had always been unduly *serious.*

"It's just fiction, Julia. By a 'fictitious' author."

"What do you mean, 'fictitious'?"

"I mean that 'Jack of Spades' is a pseudonym, as you know."

"You said you didn't know him. The author."

"I don't *know him*. It's possible that 'Jack of Spades' is a woman, in fact."

Julia laughed. "Oh no, Daddy. 'Jack of Spades' is male—sick-macho. No doubt about that."

Sick-macho. I felt a stirring of guilt, but also pride that I could disguise myself so thoroughly. My own family could not recognize me!

I assured Julia that she was exaggerating the coincidence. Best to toss the offensive novel away, and forget it.

"Could it really be a coincidence, Daddy? That's all?"

"That's all."

"So strange! I hate it."

"Well. I do, too."

"This 'Jack of Spades' is no one you know—you're sure?"

"Yes."

"Do you have any idea who he is?"

"It's said that he's a 'retired professional' who lives in the New York City area. He's a relatively new and very minor *noir* writer with a small following. Not worth your concern, Julia."

"He's a vicious person, you can tell."

"Really? I've never been able to get through one of his novels, which his publishers send to me for blurbs. They're so crude, violent—evil isn't sufficiently punished. Like action films for teenaged boys."

"Oh no, I don't think so, Daddy. Not teenaged boys. These are novels to make you *think*—but not nice thoughts."

Julia spoke shrewdly. This was an astonishing revelation to come from her, which I was reluctant to believe.

Julia persisted: "What I think, Daddy, is that this writer is someone who knows you, and our family. He based the 'accident' in *A Kiss Before Killing* on what happened to me. I just feel so *weird*."

"Julia, many people are certain that they're in works of fiction. It's like seeing a reflection in a mirror, believing it's you when it isn't."

My smile felt twisted as a corkscrew, burrowing into my face.

"Daddy, come on! If you stood in front of a mirror and saw a reflection, it would *be you*."

Julia laughed. But why was this funny?

I had only the vaguest memory of *A Kiss Before Killing*. I don't even know how it ends. I wanted to protest to Julia—*But in actual life, I am your loving father. And you did not die, after all.*

8 "I Will Have Justice"

And then, on Monday morning I could not stay away from the hearing after all.

I know, I had promised Elliot Grossman. He'd advised me expressly, more than once, to stay away. But I could not.

I was too anxious to remain at home. The fearful thought came to me that Grossman had misinterpreted the summons and *Andwer J. Rash* would be expected to be in the courtroom after all, under penalty of arrest for contempt of court.

And partly, I was obsessively curious about *C. W. Haider*. No one had ever issued a formal complaint against me for anything, let alone "theft" and "plagiarism." I had been awake much of the night miserably anticipating the hearing. *I had to see the enemy.*

Hecate County Municipal Court is a handsome old limestone building retaining most of its original eighteenth-century facade though totally renovated inside. Almost, the courthouse resembles an old church, set amid a grassy square you might expect to be a churchyard. The interior suggests a tastefully decorated private club or historic inn with mahogany-paneled walls, white-plaster ceilings, dark tile floors, recessed lighting. Unlike the abrasive and amplified atmosphere of a large urban courthouse, the atmosphere here is subdued, courteous.

Since court hearings and cases are open to the public I was not required to present ID at security. The line moved forward affably and without haste and it was a great relief, *no one recognized me.*

The courtroom in which the hearing was held was a small amphitheater the size of a moot court holding only six rows of seats which (as I rapidly calculated) could contain a maximum of seventy-two persons; by the time Judge Carson entered the courtroom, and proceedings began, this space was scarcely one-quarter filled. In the first two or three rows individuals summoned to the court and their legal counsel were seated; as hearings were adjudicated individuals left the courtroom, and others entered. Though the atmosphere was formal there was a continuous coming-and-going; those of us who'd taken spectator-seats in the last row had a clear view of the entire room.

(Trying not to appear self-conscious, or suspicious, I made it a point of not glancing around at others in my row and partially shielding my face. Indeed, like some characters created by Jack of Spades who never went out in public except in some sort of disguise, however minimal, I was wearing prescription sunglasses with heavy black frames that subtly distorted my features as well as a beige seersucker sport coat plucked from the back of my closet, which I had not worn for probably twenty years. For I was in dread of the local media "covering" this pathetic hearing, and Andrew J. Rush exposed as a thief and a plagiarist, or worse.)

Haider v. Rush was the third case on the docket. While the first two cases were being adjudicated I had time to figure out who Elliot Grossman was—a "New York"–looking (i.e., Jewish) lawyer who might've recognized me from author photographs if he'd glanced around the room, which he did not. I had time to contemplate the distinctive-looking woman who was seated conspicuously by herself in the front row, directly below the judge's bench.

No doubt, this was "C. W. Haider"—the complainant. It was uncanny how, at a first glance, she resembled a white-haired Ayn Rand, with that writer's mannish features and jutting jaw and an air both aristocratic and aggrieved. She appeared to be in her mid- or late sixties with wild white crimped hair barely tamped down by a maroon beret, and expensive looking though ill-fitting clothing of a bygone era: shoulders padded to give her frame a muscular bulk, a gray pin-striped pants suit with double lapels and large bone buttons, leather shoes with stubby toes. She had taken possession of more than one-third of the first row, having spread out to discourage others.

In profile, C. W. Haider resembled a predator bird. If she'd cast her gaze about the courtroom I would have shrunk away guiltily.

As the first of the cases was taken up, C. W. Haider made no attempt to disguise her impatience. Conspicuously she sighed and muttered to herself, shifting in her seat, rummaging amid her things—an ungainly large reptile-skin handbag, an even larger tote bag comprised of panels of a shimmering metallic material, a stack of manila folders and a single four-foot cardboard file.

Her restlessness verged upon rudeness and drew sharp frowns of annoyance from Judge Carson; it was clear that the bailiff and other courtroom staff knew the wild-white-haired Ms. Haider though in her haughtiness she didn't condescend to know them.

Grossman had told me, over the phone, that so far as he could determine, Ms. Haider had no attorney—"Probably, she hadn't been able to hire anyone for such a ridiculous case"—and so would be acting as her own attorney which would be sure to further exasperate Judge Carson.

(Though I hadn't thought initially that I knew Owen Carson, a longtime judge in Hecate County, in fact the two of us were tangentially acquainted—our wives had both served on the same Harbourton Public Library fund-raiser gala committee and were, to a degree, friends; certainly I had shaken Owen Carson's hand more than once, and seemed to recall a gratifying remark of Irina's, or Mrs. Carson's—*Owen is an admirer of your work. He loves mystery fiction though he forgets it all almost as soon as he finishes reading it!*)

By the time *Haider v. Rush* was at last called, at 10:58 A.M., Ms. Haider was in a state of pent-up frustration and ire. Excitedly she rose to her feet—(she was a surprisingly short, squat-bodied and compact woman whom padded shoulders and the dull gray pants suit did not flatter)—and identified herself to the judge as the plaintiff—"The *plain-tiff* "—as one who'd been "*stolen from for years*"—"*plagia-rized*"—in a petulant, nasal, childish voice immediately recognizable to me as the voice on the telephone.

It was evident that Judge Carson was acquainted with the plaintiff. When he inquired of her, carefully, courteously, if she did not have an attorney to represent her, Ms. Haider responded in a vehement outburst, "Sir, *I do not have an attorney because I do not want or need an attorney and because no one can speak for me. I have justice on my side this time as last time. You will see.*"

Through the courtroom, a ripple of surprise, amusement. The staid proceedings were livened as if someone had switched a TV volume on high. Coolly and courteously Judge Carson reprimanded the white-haired woman for calling him *sir* and not *Your Honor*; and the white-haired woman said snappishly, "'Honor' is something that must be earned, sir. We will see if your court deserves it."

You could see at once—(I could see at once)—that Ms. Haider's case was a lost cause, as Ms. Haider herself was a lost cause: a crank whose right to file a legal complaint against a fellow citizen was being humored *pro forma* in the courtroom but would be dismissed by the grim-faced judge as quickly as possible.

I had caught the remark—*This time as last time*. Haider had been a plaintiff in this courtroom before.

At once, I was feeling relieved. C. W. Haider was a madwoman, as I'd thought. She could not prevail over *me*.

Even Elliot Grossman, the big-city lawyer presenting the world-famous publishing house, had difficulty with Haider, who interrupted him before he could complete a sentence; several times Judge Carson resorted to using his gavel with the frustration of a TV judge trying to restore order in a comically rogue courtroom. Spectators who'd been semi-dozing through previous hearings were awake now and greatly entertained.

Indignant Ms. Haider seemed not to possess what might be called a normal or conventional sense of public behavior. The woman hadn't a clue, or disdained such, for how grating her voice was, how annoying and exasperating her superior manner; how she was sabotaging her case by her failure to conform to courtroom procedure. Even as exasperated Judge Carson was ruling her out of order she continued to speak loudly as if making herself heard was all that mattered—as if she were appealing to a justice higher than the justice of Hecate County Municipal Court. "Sir—I mean, 'Your Honor'—I have come here as a citizen to seek damages and an injunction against further theft, plagiarism, and invasion of privacy by that scoundrel 'Andrew J. Rush' who doesn't have the courage to confront me today but chooses to *hide behind a lawyer*. I will prove my case against 'Andrew J. Rush' and *I will have justice*."

It was to Judge Carson's credit that he allowed Haider to present the rudiments of a case instead of dismissing at once as another, less gentlemanly judge might have done. With the indulgence of a slightly younger relative to an elder—(Carson was in his late fifties, perhaps: with a shiny-bald head, mild myopic eyes)—he allowed the incensed plaintiff to speak at length, and to display a battery of "evidence" she'd brought with her—yellowed, typewritten manuscripts; a dozen ledger-sized journals; several copies of books of mine, with passages annotated in red. (It was a shock, before Haider identified the books, to see the dust jacket covers at a distance, and to recognize them; to realize that these were indeed *my books*—as if a portion of my private life were being exposed in the courtroom by someone bent upon destroying me.) The typed manuscripts were identified by Haider as "not-yet-published" stories and chapters from novels of *works-in-progress* by C. W. Haider; the journals were hers, dating back to 1965, when the plaintiff was eighteen years old; the hardcover books were indeed by Andrew J. Rush, containing heavily annotated passages that, Haider was claiming, had been "stolen" from her.

In a high-pitched theatrical voice Haider read passages from her material, and then passages from Andrew J. Rush—"You see? This is 'theft'—'plagi-rism.' Not only is the scoundrel stealing my words but he is stealing from my *life*."

These wild accusations went on for some time. How painful it would have been if I'd been seated at the defense table with Elliot Grossman! As it was, my eyes filled with tears of mortification. I had heard audio books of my novels read by sympathetic professionals but I had never heard my prose read aloud in such an accusatory and derisive way; the carefully constructed phrases, the "clever" similes, the unusual words (*claustral, sere*) selected from my battered old *Writer's Thesaurus* now seemed to me pathetic, self-conscious preening. Not only was Haider accusing me of plagiarizing her prose but the prose itself, exposed to the bemused audience in the courtroom, was achingly bad.

Haider's voice rose shrilly: "As these works of C. W. Haider he has pillaged have not yet been published it is clear that the scoundrel broke into my house, that is to say my late father

Walter Haider's house, at 88 Tumbrel Place, to steal them by some photocopying device . . ."

In the courtroom, ripples of laughter. What a nightmare!

Grossman was right, it had been a terrible mistake to come here. I thought—*It was Jack of Spades who brought me here.* In the future I must avoid giving in to the impulsive and anarchic impulses of Jack of Spades.

At last Judge Carson cut the plaintiff off in mid-sentence, noting that she had made her point several times. He urged Grossman to respond—"Concisely, please."

It was Grossman's contention that the case was absurd *prima facie*—the defendant Andrew J. Rush was a "distinguished, long-established master of the mystery genre" whose published work dated back to the late 1980s; Rush was the "bestselling author" of twenty-eight mystery novels translated into that many, or more, languages; indeed, Rush was a local citizen known for his civic involvement and his philanthropy. If there appeared to be "parallels" and "echoes" of the plaintiff's prose in Rush's prose, as the plaintiff had read it to the court, it was not clear that the plaintiff's prose preceded the defendant's prose, for the plaintiff had not published her work, and could offer no provable dates of composition. "Theft of a private life" could hardly be proven in any case, for nothing in Rush's novels was *evidently, obviously,* or *literally* traceable to the plaintiff's private life; if there were "coincidences" that was all that they were—"coincidences." Thus, Grossman moved to dismiss.

Furiously Haider objected that the journals were indeed "dated"—by her; and a scientific laboratory could "date" the manuscripts if there was any doubt. Grossman retorted that the journals were only dated "in the plaintiff's own hand"—and until a reputable scientific laboratory dated the manuscripts precisely, the plaintiff had not even the glimmering of a case. Again, he moved to dismiss the case as a nuisance suit, not worthy of serious judicial consideration.

Haider was becoming increasingly excited. The beret had slipped from her head and her air of superiority was unraveling. Judge Carson, whose courteous manner she'd taken for granted, as her due, was no longer so indulgent, interrupting her with his gavel, and ruling repeatedly against her, insisting that she allow Grossman to speak. Yet Haider seemed unable to keep from interrupting Grossman as if a demon were speaking through her: "No! No, no! This is *my writing*, sir! I am a writer, too—I am a writer of prose and poetry! He has *broken and entered* my residence—for years!"—"These are my precious memories, Your Honor, for this *happened to me*"—"The plagiarist takes my precious memories from me, and things that happened to me, and to my family, and he twists them into his fiction so that *it did not happen this way at all but is a nefarious LIE*."

Again Grossman moved to dismiss the "utterly flimsy, insubstantial and meretricious" case and with a single rap of his gavel Judge Carson concurred. By this point Carson was florid-faced and smarting with indignation and Haider had grown so excited, and so disheveled, the bailiff and a county sheriff's deputy hurried forward to escort her from the courtroom.

"You will please leave the courtroom peaceably, Ms. Haider. At once."

"Sir, I am here to *be heard*. I will *have justice*. I will not leave until *I have justice*."

Somehow it happened, the (portly, middle-aged) bailiff was on the floor, and—(was this possible or did I, in the confusion of the moment, imagine it)—Haider was kicking at him with her stubby-toed shoes, as one might kick at a recalcitrant door to open it.

Haider was pushing at restraining hands—a half-dozen hands by this time. Haider was screaming, and Haider was shrieking. Yellowed manuscripts fell to the floor, the cardboard file was upended—papers, documents, journals fell in a cascade. Hardcover books by Andrew J. Rush were kicked underfoot. It appeared that Haider was suffering some sort of attack, like an epileptic fit; several uniformed officers were trying to restrain her. Did I imagine it, the afflicted woman's eyes had rolled back in her head, her distended mouth was wet with saliva like the froth of madness . . . In a loud voice Judge Carson declared the morning's session closed. Hurriedly he left the room by a rear door. Poor man! I could see the abject horror in his face. The judge of a small suburban court is not accustomed to *brute, physical reality*—only to words. But now, words had erupted into *brute, physical reality.*

We were being ordered to vacate the courtroom. With others I filed out into the corridor even as the wild-white-haired woman screamed and sobbed at the front of the room, still scuffling with deputies—*Justice! I will have—justice!*

It is rare to hear the sound of madness. The actual, tearing-at-the-heart sound of another's madness.

You see? The enemy was defeated.

If more punishment is required, more punishment will be exacted.

9   Victor

On the phone, Grossman was triumphant.

"A total victory, Andrew! Maybe you should've been there, it was quite a performance."

"Was it!"—I managed to sound surprised, just slightly apprehensive.

"I mean, the plaintiff gave quite a performance. Poor woman is deranged as we'd thought." But Grossman laughed in exhilaration.

I was driving home when Grossman called my cell phone to tell me the good news. Seeing his name in the caller ID I'd been reluctant to answer with a childish fear that, though I knew better, the court case had turned out badly for me after all.

The entire episode in the courtroom had been dreamlike and unreal. Truly there was something nightmarish about the wild-white-haired C. W. Haider who'd been not only defeated but humiliated in a public place. I could hear the poor woman's cries and sobs, her demands for justice.

I thought—*But I am not responsible for any of this. She brought this disaster on herself.*

"The judge dismissed as I knew he would. He let the complainant present her ridiculous case—gave her plenty of rope to hang herself. As I thought, 'C. W. Haider' turned out to be a local crank—not looking for money, I think—so much as some kind of public apology from you, and what she calls 'damages.' Evidently she's from a well-known local family and has money, or rather has inherited money. You'd have been amused, Andrew—she was claiming that you, a bestselling writer, had actually broken into her house and stolen her writing—*literally*! You'd stolen ideas and prose passages from her manuscripts and from her journals—it looked like thousands of pages of handwritten journals. Jesus! Of course she had no proof of anything—just seemed to think that people should take her word for it. The way she addressed the court, you'd have thought she was some sort of royalty. Her major claim was that some manuscripts she'd written predated your novels—which were 'derived' from them—but there was no way to date the manuscripts, even if anyone wanted to take her ridiculous claims seriously. Unsurprisingly she's a writer who has never been published except by a few vanity presses. She's been writing a *work-in-progress* for decades. She was also claiming that you'd stolen events from her life—either you've written about her life literally, or you've changed it so much that it's a 'nefarious lie.'" Grossman laughed heartily. Through a buzzing in my ears I heard only part of what he was saying but I understood his reiterated words—*deranged, pathetic, crazy, dismissed.*

"Essentially the case is finished, Andrew. Your role is finished—you can forget about 'C. W. Haider.' I will apply for an injunction to keep her from harassing you further, and I will demand that the complainant pay legal fees and court costs. Though you're not paying my fee, and the publishing house has me on retainer, it's always a good idea to sue people like Haider for all that you can, to discourage them from initiating lawsuits. Imagine, if the case had gone to a jury, and some paranoid crank on the jury connected with Haider—it could have turned out badly for you." Grossman was working himself up to righteous indignation now. I'd had to pull over to the side of the road to listen to him.

Dazedly, I'd left the courthouse avoiding all eyes, hoping that no one would recognize me. Hearing my prose read aloud in that grating jeering voice had been lacerating. Especially, I'd made a point of avoiding Elliot Grossman who was lingering on the courthouse steps talking animatedly with fellow lawyers—an assertive individual, very New York in manner, flush with victory and feeling the anticlimax of the abrupt dismissal. Grossman had been brought by limousine all the way from midtown Manhattan to Harbourton, New Jersey, and was finished with his day's work before 2:00 P.M.—still supercharged with adrenaline.

By the time I'd left the courthouse parking lot, I had heard a siren—I'd seen an ambulance pull up to the front entrance. A small crowd had gathered on the walk in front of the building, parting just enough to allow medical workers to hurry through.

I'd looked quickly away. I hadn't wanted to see even a glimpse of the stricken white-haired woman.

But if you are very lucky, she will die now.
She will die, and you will never be exposed.

In his cruel jubilant voice Grossman was boasting again of how well the case had gone, exactly as he'd anticipated. Was he expecting me to praise him? Thank him—again?

"Something for you to write about in one of your thrillers, eh, Andrew?"

I felt the sting of insult. As if I had nothing better to write about than the pathetic C. W. Haider!

Through a haze of headache pain, I thanked Grossman. I praised him, and I assured him that I would tell my editor how brilliantly he'd handled the case, but—"I don't think that we should pursue the plaintiff further. Let's drop the pathetic case now."

"What do you mean, 'let it drop'? I don't understand."

"I don't want to sue her for—whatever you'd said: fees, court costs. Let's just let it drop."

"Andrew, the plaintiff lost her case and she should pay costs. She should pay for her recklessness in bringing suit. Why should your publisher pay?"

"I'll pay. I'll pay your fee and whatever the costs are. Just send me a bill."

"Don't be ridiculous. You're the innocent party. My fee is paid by the publishing house. And I am well paid. But Haider is the losing party, and she *should pay*. Fees are deterrents in nuisance cases. Otherwise every idiot would be suing every other idiot and the courts would be jammed. This woman comes from a well-to-do family, after all."

I insisted, I didn't want to further humiliate C. W. Haider. She was hospitalized—was she? She'd collapsed in the courtroom, and had to be taken away by ambulance . . .

"How do you know that, Andrew?"

"You told me."

"Did I? I don't remember telling you."

Perspiration broke out on my forehead, and inside my clothes. My head throbbed with pain. I could not recall whether Grossman had told me any of this.

"Yes, you said—you told me that Haider had collapsed in the courtroom and an ambulance was called. Just a few minutes ago, you told me this."

"Did I?"—it seemed that Grossman was genuinely perplexed.

Quickly I stammered that I had to hang up, I couldn't drive while talking on the phone and would speak with him another time.

It was several minutes before I felt strong enough, and my scattered thoughts focused enough, for me to drive the rest of the way home to Mill Brook House.

I entered the house, which was very quiet. I hadn't noticed if Irina's car was in the driveway. No one appeared to be home.

Not even the cleaning woman. No one.

Silence rolled at me, in waves.

They are all dead, and you are free.

And you are blameless.

10 "Spotless As a Lamb"

And then, I waited.

The *Harbourton Weekly* came out on Wednesdays.

Stealing myself for a withering front-page headline *Local Author Rush Sued for Theft, Plagiarism in Hecate Co. Court.*

There were no stories about the events of Monday on local TV or radio. No reporters tried to contact me. Nor did Irina seem to know that something upsetting had occurred in my life, and of course I didn't tell her.

When at last the *Weekly* was delivered to our mailbox, and I opened it hurriedly, I saw nothing on the front page that bore my name or photograph. No *Rush*, no *Haider*.

Slowly I walked back to the house. My hands were trembling and my eyes filled with moisture.

In sudden dread I stopped to open the *Weekly*, to scan the "Court Beat" column on page six, even the "Police Blotter"— nothing.

Through the entire paper, nothing.

My heart lifted. I laughed aloud, in gratitude. I felt the euphoria of one who has escaped punishment, though I could not have said why.

11   Perfect Crime

And now, it is time.

  For Andrew J. Rush to commit a perfect crime.

In the night waking with a lurch of my heart. And my jaws aching as if I'd been grinding my back teeth.

What time was it?—barely I could make out the numerals on the bedside clock.

That time before dawn that is not-yet-dawn. The Hour of the Wolf it is called, when people who are gravely ill are most susceptible to death.

Can't you see? In front of your eyes?

Your enemy—helpless.

Your enemy—waiting.

On the farther side of the bed Irina was sleeping. Since moving to Mill Brook House we'd acquired a "king-sized" bed vast as a field in which two living breathing heat-producing bodies can lie oblivious of each other through the night.

Though sometimes, it is true that Irina will call out to me, "Andrew? Are you all right?"

Or, "Andrew? Are you having a bad dream?"

Or, "Andrew! You were grinding your teeth again."

This time, Irina wasn't (evidently) awake. Something had roused me from sleep at the climax of a dream of such chaos and confusion I'd immediately forgotten it—or rather, whatever it had been, *possibly, fleetingly, involving the wild-white-haired woman*—I was no longer able to recall.

It was in such ways, at such times, that Jack of Spades most directly spoke to me. But I wasn't always sure what Jack of Spades meant by his taunting words.

. . . *time.*

. . . *perfect crime.*

12   Temptation

"Andrew? May I have a minute?"

It was Grossman. I had not wanted to answer the phone but felt compelled out of duty.

A week had passed since the hearing in the Hecate County courthouse. My dread of being exposed in the local media was abating slowly and I was back to work, or nearly. Still I checked my e-mail with trepidation, and rarely answered the phone unless I recognized the caller as someone whom I knew well and could trust.

I'd hoped not to hear from my publisher's lawyer again. The episode had been upsetting in ways I could not have explained. So far as I was concerned, the case was over.

I was determined not to think of C. W. Haider ever again—though at weak moments I found myself staring into space and hearing the furious wrathful voice *I will have justice!*

I wondered if the wild-white-haired woman had died in the hospital. For all I knew, she might have died of a stroke or a heart attack in the ambulance. For a fleeting moment I thought that Grossman might have been calling to tell me this and I did not know if I would feel relief, or guilty regret.

But Grossman's voice was ebullient, loud in my ear.

"Very interesting development, Andrew! Are you prepared for a surprise?"

No. No more surprises.

"I suppose so. Yes."

"Remember, I'd predicted that this C. W. Haider had to be a 'local crank'?—turns out that this is so. She has filed complaints against other writers—major writers—just as she did you. My paralegal did a little investigating, and discovered that Haider tried to sue Stephen King a few years ago. I wasn't representing King at that time but I know the attorney who worked with him, and I gave him a call, and guess what, Andrew—"

For a moment I couldn't quite comprehend.

Stephen King? She'd tried to sue—also?

Andrew J. Rush is not special to her—after all?

Grossman was saying that the case Haider had prepared against Stephen King was virtually identical to the one she'd prepared against Andrew J. Rush except for different prose passages from different books.

Even the ridiculous breaking-and-entering charge was identical.

"Imagine—the likelihood of Stephen King coming to Harbourton, New Jersey—to break into *her house.*"

Grossman laughed heartily. Indeed it was a preposterous fantasy.

"In October 2004 there'd been a hearing in the same courtroom, with Haider 'representing herself' before the same judge." This, Grossman thought particularly amusing.

Weakly, I tried to laugh. "Really! The same judge . . ."

Stephen King had been so alarmed by the woman, who'd also written threatening letters to him in care of his publisher, that he'd hired a private detective to investigate her. He'd been afraid that she might drive to Maine and stalk him and his family— afraid that she was crazy enough to try to kill someone. But the detective hadn't turned up much that sounded dangerous, so King dropped the case.

"You're sure she has never written you threatening letters, Andrew? Maybe they went to the publisher, and didn't get forwarded."

I had no idea how to reply to this. I was feeling mildly stunned and could not think coherently. Grossman's ebullient laughter seemed to be suffocating me.

"Your adversary has also tried to sue, over the years, John Updike and John Grisham, Norman Mailer and Dean Koontz, Peter Straub and James Patterson—*and* Dan Brown!—all without success."

We laughed together. Well, this was funny—wasn't it?

Slowly I was deflating. Like a balloon that has been pierced by a pin.

"Quite a virtuoso, your 'Ms. Haider'! Impressive range of styles and themes."

"Yes—well . . . I guess it shouldn't be a surprise."

It is a total surprise. And not a flattering surprise.

"So, Andrew, I'd like to file a complaint against *her*. As I'd said, the next step should be ours."

I understood, this was probably so. A lawyer would know, and would have my best interests at heart. Grossman was only being reasonable and yet, my instinct was to resist.

"But—do you know how she is? It's possible that she isn't even alive . . ."

"My paralegal made inquiries. She was taken to New Brunswick for 'observation'—she may have some sort of congenital epileptic condition, that causes her to throw fits when she's frustrated or angry. There's a family caretaker with whom my paralegal spoke, who was very helpful. He told the paralegal that 'fighting her enemies' was what kept Ms. Haider going after her father died and she was left alone in the world. Not just her literary enemies but neighbors on Tumbrel Place and town officials. Incidentally, she's sixty-seven years old."

Sixty-seven! I'd hoped she was older. This seemed dismayingly young. With the steely resolve of the mad, C. W. Haider could be my nemesis for the next twenty years.

"If you don't disapprove, Andrew, I'm going to move ahead with my plans. We'll get an injunction against her to 'cease and desist harassing' you and we'll file for charges. You don't have to be involved except to sign a document or two."

But still I felt an instinct to resist, to demur. In this unpleasant situation, Andrew J. Rush had to behave *nobly.*

"I've told you, Elliot—I don't want to be punitive. This incident has left a sour taste in my mouth."

"But you've been the victim! Imagine if you didn't have a publisher who was willing to protect you, and you'd had to hire a lawyer—a Manhattan, not a Harbourton, New Jersey, lawyer. (I don't come cheaply, Andrew—which is why you should follow my counsel.) Imagine if the local judge hadn't been reasonable, and the case had gone to trial. Imagine if the judgment had gone against you, who knows what the settlement might've been—millions? You'd have to appeal to the New Jersey State Court of Appeals—none of this a bargain, I can tell you. More bizarre and unjust things have happened in the history of US law."

"But—what exactly would you do? How much would she have to pay?"

Patiently Grossman explained his plans another time. He estimated a sum—far more than I'd anticipated.

"I told you, Andrew *we'll bury her.*"

For a moment I felt this temptation. It was like creeping out onto a diving board—a high diving board—to (gently, almost unobtrusively)—press against the bare back of another, to urge him into space.

A temptation to give in to the aggressive lawyer's advice, to sue and to punish. To further defeat the enemy. *Bury her.*

But I heard myself say:

"I understand, Elliot. But—I still don't want to sue."

"Jesus! Are you some sort of—Christian? Quaker? Is it fair to your publisher, to expect the company to pay?"

"I've told you, I will pay the fees and the costs myself. I just want to forget this sorry episode, and get back to my life."

"Well—that's very noble of you. Gentlemanly."

(Was Grossman sneering? I could imagine his mouth twitching in disdain.)

"I feel sorry for the woman, that's all. Mental illness isn't a choice or an option, and it shouldn't be confused with criminal behavior. From Haider's point of view, she believed that she was right."

"Exactly what one might have said about Hitler, or Genghis Khan. Our own war criminal politicians. Quite right."

"Haider isn't a Hitler or a Genghis Khan. She's a lonely old woman who imagines she's a writer. She may be permanently disabled, after her stroke. I just don't want to make things more desperate for her, it was enough to win the case."

"Very well, Andrew. We'll let it go. For now, at least."

"I don't want this to continue any longer, please. I'd be terribly ashamed if anyone knew we were persecuting this woman. I don't intend to give 'C. W. Haider' another thought."

"Good! It's rare that the object of a lawsuit is so generous, but 'Andrew J. Rush' is obviously not an ordinary man. Can you promise not to contact her, at least? In the hospital or at home?"

"Of course! I have no reason to contact her."

"You've told me already that you did contact her, by phone."

"That was to appeal to her, to drop the complaint. I don't have any reason to contact her again."

"Well—you might imagine that you could convince her you're 'innocent.' You don't seem to realize that 'innocence' isn't the point in the law—it's what the law determines that establishes 'innocence' or 'guilt.' Whether you stole every one of your twenty-eight novels from C. W. Haider's shelf of manuscripts, or not a single line, doesn't matter; it's only what the judge has ruled that matters. What other people, like the litigious C. W. Haider, might think is of zero significance."

This was damned insulting but I forced myself to murmur in assent.

"Maybe we'll speak again. I hate to leave it like this. As a professional, I think my advice is valuable to my client—it isn't just a matter of sentiment. At least, promise me that you'll steer clear of the woman."

"Of course, I won't. I mean—I won't try to contact her."

"And if she harasses you again, call me immediately."

"Yes."

"D'you promise? You will cell me immediately, if she gives you trouble again."

"Yes. I will call you immediately."

"And what I'll do, Andrew, is hit her with all I've got. No more Mr. Nice Guy, eh? *We will bury her.*"

That night I was in bed fairly by midnight. Too exhausted even to take up my pen and yellow legal pad and sit sipping whiskey at the battered little table immersed in the seductive prose of Jack of Spades.

But I slept only intermittently. Sighing, and squirming, like a great fish caught in a net.

And who is wielding the net?

13   Immunity

You have immunity now.
No one will believe the witch if she accuses you.

Frequently Jack of Spades teased.

Frequently Jack of Spades taunted.

In the interstices of my "own" life—my writing-life as Andrew J. Rush—the sibilant words sounded like leaking gas.

Especially in my attractive study built above the old stable. In what had been my place of refuge I felt vulnerable, edgy.

Anything you wish to do, C.W. is your target.

See what is before your eyes! The most delicious challenge.

"I have absolutely no interest in C. W. Haider. I am not even going to make inquiries about her health."

This was so. This was my resolve.

In the weeks following the summons, and the hearing. In the weeks following the collapse in the courtroom. The screams.

Jus-tice!

Yet it seemed that my work was not going well. The meticulous twenty-page outline of *Criss-Cross* suddenly did not make sense. Much of my work-time was spent listlessly rereading, revising. Before the summons, I had been at approximately page 120 of the novel but now, with daily corrosion, I had barely half that much that I could bear to read.

All that I'd labored diligently at, through the crisis, now rang hollow in my ears. My prose, mocked by the wild-white-haired woman in the courtroom, was revealed as flat and unconvincing. My "characters" whom I had, I'd thought, lovingly created, and whose pencil-drawn likenesses were tacked to the corkboard beside my table, seemed to have conspired against me, behind my back, to utter empty banalities of the sort you see in cartoons.

You see?—the witch has put a curse upon you.

What will you do, to exorcise it?

14   "Nephew"

She'd been transferred to a psychiatric clinic in New Brunswick. I knew, I'd made more than one discreet call.

"Would you like to speak with Ms. Haider, sir? She's in the dayroom right now, I can see her from here."

Quickly I told the nurse no. No thank you. I didn't want to upset my aunt.

"Ms. Haider wouldn't be upset, I think. She's been lonely. She has been making excellent progress here but it's very helpful if a patient has visitors. Especially, older patients need to 'connect' with familiar faces to keep them from delusional thoughts. Did you say that you are Ms. Haider's nephew?"

Explaining that yes, I was Ms. Haider's nephew, but only the son of a stepbrother of hers, living in Duluth, Iowa—(but was Duluth in Iowa?)—and too far away to come visit her at the present time.

"Well, we're hoping Ms. Haider will be an outpatient soon. She's the brightest and most talkative patient here right now. 'Course, she's got a lot to grumble about, it seems. Sure is a *grumbler.*" The nurse laughed, as if her remark were some sort of understatement, which I, as a relative, might appreciate.

"So—my aunt is making progress? She'll be discharged soon?"

"Yes, sir. What's your name? I will tell her you called."

"Stephen. My name is Stephen."

"'Stephen'—Haider?"

"No. Stephen King."

There was a startled silence. Then, "You mean—like the writer? The same name as the famous writer?"

"The same name, yes. But not the same person."

"Well—good! I will tell Ms. Haider you are thinking of her, Mr. King!"

"Call me Stephen, please."

"*Stephen.* Gosh!"

15   "I Like Not That"

"If you don't mind, Andrew. I think I should attend . . ."

Hesitantly Irina spoke. Between us was the issue of Irina's hours at the Friends School, which seemed to me excessive for the (modest) salary she received.

"Most of the staff will be there . . . I won't stay for the buffet supper."

"Don't be silly, darling! If you want to, you should."

"Well, I don't *want to*. I *want to* have dinner with my husband of course . . ."

To placate my dear wife who was looking apologetic, in a way that was both touching and annoying, I told Irina that she should certainly stay for supper with her colleagues, at the headmaster's house. It would seem rude, or perhaps unprofessional, or might cause them to think she was less committed to her job than others if she rushed home to her husband whom she saw (after all) seven days a week. I would use the opportunity to have dinner with a (recently divorced) friend in Harbourton.

In addition, I would drop by the Harbourton library, to donate a box of books that had accumulated over the summer. Several times a year I donated books to the local library, that were sent to me by publishers; not always, but sometimes, I used the occasion to donate a paperback or two by Jack of Spades whose novels, I'd noticed, were not purchased by the library.

(Once, I'd made an inquiry about this omission to the head librarian who was an old friend and she'd said, with a crinkle of her nose, "Oh, well—we don't purchase books like that." But I saw that no one at the library seemed to mind if Jack of Spades was donated, to be displayed on the Mystery Paperbacks shelf alongside such hallowed rivals as Michael Connelly, James Ellroy, Mary Higgins Clark, and, indeed, Andrew J. Rush.)

When Irina was hired to teach art at the Friends School in Hadrian, she'd been very happy and I had been happy for her. Since the children left home she'd tried with varying degrees of success to work on her own art, such as it was—landscape watercolors, glazed ceramics, macramé—but there was nothing quite like teaching to invigorate her. Irina also had our house and property to maintain, which she enjoyed, and on which she spent a considerable amount of money—(of course, with my approval); she was generous with her time at local charitable organizations, and served on various fund-raising committees. There is no term that so sinks the heart of a husband as *fund-raiser*—but I have tried to be supportive of her in these efforts. I have always wanted my dear wife, who is inclined to emotional moods and "melancholia," to be productively happy.

At the same time, I don't want Irina's good nature to be exploited by others.

"If anyone is going to exploit you, darling, it should be *me*."

With a little wince Irina laughed. I leaned over to kiss her warm cheek and felt her stiffen just slightly for Irina does not always like my jocular side, as she describes it.

When we'd first met at Rutgers, as undergraduates, it had certainly seemed that we were equals; in fact, Irina's grades were higher than mine. In our writing workshops, which we'd happened to take together, it was Irina Kacinzk with her "poetic" prose in the mode of Virginia Woolf whom the other writers and our instructor most admired, and not Andy Rush whose Hemingway-derived stories were flatly written, awkwardly earnest, and plot-driven with melodramatic "action" scenes and Hollywood-type dialogue. The first story of Irina's I'd read, about a deaf, dumb, and blind girl, brilliantly evoked and convincing, made a powerful impression on me. I'd thought, with the naïveté of a nineteen-year-old—*Here is the girl I will marry.*

It did not matter to me that, in our workshop, Irina was often too shy to speak; and that, among other young women at Rutgers, she was not strikingly attractive or sexually provocative, but rather quietly appealing, with ashy blond hair, wire-rimmed glasses, intense eyes. An intelligent person—obviously. The kind of person who must be cultivated, to be appreciated and who is, if female, grateful for the interest of one with a stronger personality than her own.

Of the numerous girls I'd known, none had seemed to be so impressed with me as Irina. In her eyes the *Andy Rush* who was reflected scarcely seemed, at times, to be *me*.

"Irina? Call me 'Andy,' please."

"'I think that I would rather call you 'Andrew.'"

This was flattering, somehow. For everyone I knew called me "Andy"—a name comfortable as an old sneaker. There was dignity in "Andrew," and a kind of depth, complexity. Perhaps I began to fall in love with Irina Kacinzk for seeing more in me than I saw in myself at the time.

Of course, from time to time, Irina has called me "Andy." In her most affectionate moments, when she feels comfortable in my love, she even calls me "dear"—"darling."

But it is "Andrew" that is most natural to her for it seems to suggest a slight distance between us: "Andrew" the husband, father, protector and provider.

Soon after we were married, Irina gave up writing. I had been her most enthusiastic reader and had continued to encourage her, going through drafts of stories and novels, but something hesitant and self-doubting had crept into her sense of herself as a writer. Gently I admonished her—"Darling, you care too much for precision and perfection. There's no need to polish each damned sentence—just *say what you want to say*."

But Irina grew ever more shy about her writing. I hope it wasn't because I insisted upon reading everything she wrote, and offering my heartfelt, sincere, and sympathetic critiques.

Though we'd begun as equals, to a degree, both of us finding teaching jobs in the Highland Park area, Irina's salary from the start was less than mine; her high grades at Rutgers and the great enthusiasm of her professors didn't so much matter outside the university. Many times in those early, strained years I had to assure Irina that it didn't matter in the slightest—(indeed, it did not matter in the slightest!)—that the income she brought into the household was rarely more than 70 percent of my own, and went almost entirely for day care when the children were young.

As in a fairy tale we changed places over the years. My first serious stories, Irina helped me revise, even typed for me; it was Irina who provided ideas for plots that weren't so far-fetched as mine, but lively and surprising; it was Irina who provided dialogue where my dialogue was flat and repetitive. Irina had written a senior honors thesis on prevailing themes in fairy tales, and these themes she'd suggested to me as concepts for my mystery novels, to give them what Irina called *gravitas*. Memorably, when she was eight months pregnant with our firstborn, Irina carefully retyped a forty-page story of mine, with corrections, and sent it to the venerable mystery magazine *Ellery Queen* where it was promptly accepted for publication.

Following that, agents began to write to Andrew J. Rush. I chose a Manhattan agent whose clients included some of the bestselling mystery writers in the country, and I have remained with this excellent agent ever since. Though my stories were frequently rejected, my first attempt at a novel—(with my dear wife's help)—was met with encouragement and enthusiasm; within two years I had a contract for another novel, with a (moderately) generous advance from a publisher with a strong mystery-crime-detective list. I was not yet thirty years old.

Since that time, I have never been without a writing project—a plan of action. And I rarely look back.

Having given up trying to write, Irina turned to "art." As I am not any sort of expert on art I am always supportive of her efforts even when I can see (I think I can see) that her watercolors are only just wanly pretty, and in no way original; so too, her glazed ceramics and her macramé are interchangeable with those executed by her women friends in the area, who take courses at the Mill Brook Valley Arts Co-op and whose houses are gradually filling with their creations, like ships gradually sinking beneath the weight of ever-more cargo.

Of course, I didn't suggest any of this to my dear wife who *tries so hard.*

Sometimes, I came upon Irina's notebooks around the house. She'd given up trying to write prose fiction but was trying to write poetry—mostly just random lines that were exquisite (I thought) but made no sense.

And sometimes too, I came upon Irina crying.

At first, Irina would deny that she was *crying.*

Just—"Sitting here thinking."

Or—"It's just nothing, just a mood. I don't really have anything to do that I want to do, I guess."

Or, after I'd questioned her—"Maybe it's some stupid thing like being lonely. Please let's forget it."

Or, suddenly, one day, wiping angrily at her eyes—"You take my ideas from me, Andrew. I don't have anything left that is my own."

This was stunning to me. Almost, I couldn't believe what I'd heard.

"Irina, that's ridiculous! I've never taken any ideas from you except those you've given me freely, that I'd thought you had wanted to give."

This was true! Irina laughed wanly, and did not disagree.

"In fact, Irina dear, you've taken ideas from *me*."

I was referring to suggestions I'd made to her to improve her watercolors. And years ago before she'd given up writing I could see (I thought that I could see) fairly obvious variants of themes, settings, even characters and dialogue appropriated from my novels though I would never have spoken of this to my dear fragile wife.

The fact was, the children were growing into adolescence, and beyond. The children did not need their mother so much any longer though it seemed, painfully at times, that their mother needed them. I insisted that Irina see a therapist—in time, a sequence of therapists. She began to write again, though she didn't show me what she was writing. (I did not inquire.) We went on vacations to St. Bart's, Paris and Nice, Rome, Florence, and Venice. We stayed for as long as two or three weeks. During such interludes I managed to get some work accomplished (for I brought my laptop and notes everywhere with me—I am nothing if not industrious!) while Irina spent time sightseeing, taking photographs, befriending other tourists.

When we returned, Irina seemed quite energized, for a while. But soon she began to lapse into her moods—her "melancholia."

But teaching at the Friends School was rejuvenating to Irina, at least. Though the private school paid a paltry salary and seemed to exult in its very "specialness"—its quasi-amateur faculty grateful for their jobs in a worthwhile mission. Those colleagues of Irina's whom I'd met seemed like unusually dedicated people— mostly women. But the headmaster was male, with an impressive degree from Princeton; and Irina's particular friend at the school was an Asian-born math teacher with an unpronounceable name resembling "Huang Lee."

I'd met "Huang Lee" just once at a Harbourton library fundraiser. It was startling to me, "Huang Lee" wasn't at all what I'd expected, a somewhat stiff and deferential Asian-American but a quick-witted individual who made his (white) listeners laugh. Irina had happened to mention to me that "Huang Lee" was one of the more popular teachers at the school and that girl students were "always falling in love with him."

At this, I had to laugh. Back at Highland Park High School, girl students were always falling in love with their English teacher Mr. Rush.

I wondered: would "Huang Lee" be at the school meeting? Would "Huang Lee" (whom I believed to be married, with young children) stay for the buffet supper?

From my octagonal study window I watched Irina drive away in the Subaru station wagon (the less glamorous of our vehicles: the other, more usually driven by me, is a new-model Jaguar). I watched her turn left at Mill Brook Road, in the direction of Hadrian six miles away. For a moment I felt a curious impulse to follow her.

I like not that.

Such phrases Jack of Spades inserted into the stream of my thoughts, that were random and inexplicable and not to be taken seriously.

I like not that. Nor should you.

16   Tumbrel Place I

Soon after Irina's departure I drove into Harbourton along our winding, narrow country roads. With a gentlemanly flourish I delivered the box of books to the library. Jody Harkness (the head librarian) wasn't there but my presence created a flurry of interest among the other librarians who called me "Mr. Rush."

"When is your next novel coming out, Mr. Rush? I hope soon!"

"Soon. Yes."

At 6:00 P.M. it was still bright as midday though the sky had been overcast since morning. I realized that I'd forgotten to make dinner plans with my friend at the Harbourton Inn.

In Harbourton, where I'd grown up, I had many friends and still many more friendly acquaintances. Yet it was beginning to be unnerving, I seemed rarely to see any of them, any longer. (I did not want to think that my old Harbourton High classmates felt uncomfortable in my presence since I'd become something of a local celebrity. And it had to be awkward for them and their wives to invite Irina and me to dinner at their modest homes, after visiting us in Mill Brook House.)

I found myself driving slowly through Harbourton. Slowly, along Chapel Street in the direction of the historic district: courthouse, post office, red-brick Episcopal church and rectory, Tumbrel Square, cobblestone cul-de-sac Tumbrel Place. In this distinguished old residential neighborhood there were few pedestrians. During the day you were likely to see lawn crews, delivery vans, postmen; in this hour of early evening, all looked deserted. This was a neighborhood of large, dignified, once-beautiful old houses set back from the street—"stately homes" built in the 1800s. The oldest could be dated to pre–Revolutionary War times, when (it was not improbable) General George Washington had been a guest beneath its steep shingled roof on his way to the Battle of Trenton.

The residence at 88 Tumbrel Place was a large, gaunt, rather ugly Edwardian house of bricks so aged they seemed bleached of color. Here was a petulant sort of dignity. The roof was luminous-green, covered thinly in moss. Tall oaks surrounding the house had been maimed by storms and were missing parts of their limbs. Though I knew that the wild-white-haired Ms. Haider could not be home yet I felt a quivering of excitement imagining that she stood at one of the second-floor windows, gazing at me as casually I drove past the house to park my car a short distance away, by the Episcopal rectory.

You have immunity now. No one will believe her.
The curse must be exorcised.

I'd come to realize that it was so, there was a kind of "curse" on me since the shock of the summons in my mailbox. Since the sight of the wild-white-haired witch-woman who'd wanted to destroy me.

Yet oddly, it seemed to me that the "curse"—a sort of free-floating, lethargic malaise, like the dank smell of a toadstool brought too close to the nostrils, that made it all but impossible for me to concentrate on my work—had fallen upon me before the arrival of the summons itself.

An enemy in my peaceful life. Of whom I had had not a clue.

Too long I'd been a trusting person. Wanting to believe the best of everyone.

Parked my Jaguar, put on old, tortoiseshell-framed eyeglasses with lenses that magnified my eyes like a fish's eyes. A grimy dark green baseball cap which I'd found by chance in the library parking lot, I pulled down tight over my head.

In the backseat of the vehicle was my dark green tote bag and a book-sized box, in which I'd placed a single quite heavy hardcover book. The box I'd wrapped in tinsel wrapping paper and decorated with a white satin bow, from my dear wife's present-wrapping closet. My heart beat quickly in anticipation. Jack of Spades laughed.

Very clever, Andrew! But we will see how you carry it off.

Unhurried, with the sauntering gait of one who lived in the shabby-genteel neighborhood, I returned to 88 Tumbrel Place carrying both the tinsel-wrapped box and my (empty) duffel bag. (To my relief, I had no impression of a ghostly white-haired figure at any of the windows.) A few blocks away on South Main Street there came a sound of traffic but here in historic Tumbrel Place it was silent as the grave.

A wrought iron gate, which required some exertion to push open. Up the weatherworn flagstones to the oaken front door, and the doorbell.

No answer. (No one inside?)

Politely then, I used the door knocker that was in the shape of an American eagle.

And again no answer.

Pondering then if I might (unobtrusively, unnoticed) saunter along a flagstone path beside the house, that led through a tunnel of overgrown shrubbery to the rear, or whether this might be unwise and reckless, when unexpectedly the door was opened, to my surprise—and there stood before me a short, squat, barrel-chested black man with upright swirls of gray hair, in a snug-fitting black gabardine coat and mismatched trousers, who greeted me with a ferocious scowl.

"Yas? What'd you want?"

Quickly I reasoned that this belligerent individual had to be Haider's caretaker. The man was so short, scarcely five feet tall, he had to crane his neck to glare up at me.

I asked if this was the Haider residence and was curtly told, "Yas. Ha'der res'dence. What'd you want?"

I explained that I was a rare book dealer from Bangor, Maine—and a publisher of high-quality books—and a writer-friend of Ms. Haider. I had brought her a "special edition book" she'd requested several months ago which only recently had I been able to "acquisition." I asked if I might give the book to Ms. Haider in person, since it was a rare, rare edition?

"Nah. Mz. Ha'der ain't seein anybody."

But the caretaker was regarding me less fiercely now. In my grimy baseball cap, with my thick-lensed glasses and gentlemanly way of speaking, it was possible to interpret me as a literary eccentric—indeed, a very plausible "writer-friend" of C. W. Haider.

I added, with a disarming smile:

"I am truly sorry to intrude on this household but—I am expected, you know. My name is King. Steven."

"'King.'" The suspicious eye's blinked. "You sayin you are that famous writer?"

"No! I am Steven—S–t–e–v–e–n. He is Stephen."

"But—you are some kind of *writer?*"

"Yes. And a publisher as well, with an interest in publishing Ms. Haider's work."

This was the inspired thing to say! The caretaker smiled broadly.

"She goin to like that, sir. I mean—Mr. King. Mz. Ha'der goin to be real happy about that."

It was touching, the black servant cared so genuinely for his employer! He introduced himself as Esdra Staples.

"'Esdra.' So good to meet you."

I extended my hand to shake his. For a startled moment he hesitated—(obviously, Esdra Staples *knew his place*)—then he shook my hand. Esdra's hand was half again as large as mine, and mine is not a small hand—remarkably strong, and warm-blooded.

"Mz. Ha'der ain't home at the present time, but I can take the book for her. I will take good care of it. She trusts me, all kinds of things."

"I think my dear friend Ms. Haider requested that the book be placed *in her hands*. It's not only a rare purchase, but has sentimental value to her."

"Well. That too bad, Mr. King. See, she ain't here."

"When will she return?"

"She ain't said." Esdra spoke guardedly. His forehead furrowed with a pained sort of solicitude.

"Well, then—where is she?"

My concern was so seemingly genuine, Esdra relented.

"Ms. Ha'der taken sick, and she being treated. Some place she goes, in New Brunswick. She be home soon, they sayin."

"Oh! Ms. Haider is *ill*?"

"She been like this before, when old Mr. Ha'der died and she was grieving. She 'checked herself in' and after a few weeks she was fine, and came back home."

"Really! That sounds—optimistic . . ."

I felt a wave of sympathy, and guilt. It had not been my fault that C. W. Haider had worked herself into a convulsive fit and collapsed but I could well understand how years of frustration, fury, and failure could drive an aspiring writer to madness and breakdown.

I explained to Esdra that Ms. Haider and I had an "epistolary" relationship exclusively—"That is, a friendship through the mail"—but had not yet met; I told him that Ms. Haider had volunteered to lend me several books from her library to help in my research into the American Gothic novel. In fact, I hoped to incorporate some of Ms. Haider's own writings in my study.

"Yah, she always writing, seems like. She gon be pleased to hear that. But she didn't tell me about anybody coming to pick up books . . ."

"If I see them, I will recognize them, Esdra. Of course."

With a touching sort of naïve trust Esdra led me into the interior of the Haider house. There were shadowy, dank-smelling rooms that appeared to be shut-off and unused. Ghostly sheets drawn over furniture, even over chandeliers. At the rear was a comfortably cluttered room containing a beautiful old mahogany desk heaped with books and papers, an aged leather sofa and cushioned chairs, a wide stone fireplace. The walls were mostly bookshelves and these were crammed with books. On the floor, an Oriental carpet worn threadbare in places and in other places retaining its intricately meshed colors. I thought—*This is her home. I have no right to intrude in the woman's home.*

On the sofa, on a quilt, lay a sleek black cat regarding me with eyes glaring like gold coins. The cat's long tail switched restlessly but the cat did not leap up and run away in alarm.

Esdra was telling me that Ms. Haider was "all the time writing"—as long as he'd been working in the household, going back to a time when her father Mr. Haider had hired him.

"See, Mz. Haider has a 'mission'—'message' to the world—she says. She been trying so hard to have a book published by some place *real*—not where the writer pays the printer. She will be very happy to see you, Mr. King . . ."

I wondered if Esdra had ever read anything by his mistress? And did he know about her "missions" of litigation? Did he know—did he suspect—that she was *not quite sane;* or rather, was his loyalty unquestioned, even as, shrewdly, he would have no wish to delve too deeply into her activities?

I wondered if C. W. Haider had no relatives, or perhaps no relatives with whom she was on friendly terms. The dignified old Edwardian house had been deteriorating for decades and the life of its household, so to speak, had retreated to a single room. Without the "caretaker"—what would become of the household, or of its mistress?

Indeed Esdra Staples did seem dwarf-like, like a servant in a fairy tale. He was compact, and short, though without the typical upper-body deformity of a dwarf. He was wearing soiled work trousers and what appeared to be a very old, ill-fitting butler's black jacket, with rolled-up cuffs. From a remark he'd made as he was leading me through the house I understood that he didn't live at Tumbrel Place but a distance away; he came to the house at least once a day, to bring in the mail, feed the cat, check that things were all right.

"I'll leave this here, Esdra. Thank you!"

I set the tinsel-wrapped box on the desk, prominently. This, Haider would see as soon as she stepped into the room.

Bringing the gift, the book, had been an inspiration out of nowhere—out of the (previous) night. I'd taken Stephen King's *Misery* from my bookshelf and "inscribed" it

To C. W. Haider with everlasting gratitude
Your friend & sincere admirer
Steve King
Bangor, Maine

I'd disguised my handwriting—of course. I'd included a little drawing of a mock-smiling face.

How incensed Haider would be, when she returned to this!

It was a cruel joke perhaps but—as Jack of Spades had pointed out—no one had forced C. W. Haider to initiate a lawsuit against King, Rush, and others.

It's her against you. She has laid a curse on you.

Esdra told me that I could look through Ms. Haider's bookshelves if I wanted to but he couldn't help much. He had work to do outside—he was clearing away tree debris from a recent storm. No matter how hard he worked, seemed like he couldn't keep up with all the things going wrong with the house, that would make Ms. Haider sad to see when she returned . . .

I thanked Esdra and told him that I was fine looking through the books on the shelves and that I didn't need his assistance.

While the loyal caretaker was clearing away debris with a rake I could observe him through a window, through a thatch work of overgrown vines. But I did not think that the loyal caretaker could see me.

Her against you. No mercy.

"My God!"

From a shelf I pulled two old, indeed antiquated volumes— Mary Shelley's *Frankenstein, or the Modern Prometheus.* The pages were desiccated and the bindings badly worn but the date was 1823—a true collector's item. I had no idea what such an edition would cost in today's market but supposed it was well beyond the price of my entire "first edition" library at Mill Brook House.

Beside the *Frankenstein* volumes was an equally antiquated copy of *The Last Man,* 1826, signed by Mary Shelley; beside this, volumes by Bram Stoker—*Dracula* (1897), *The Lady of the Shroud* (1909), *The Lair of the White Worm* (1911). All were signed by Bram Stoker, the inked signature faded but still legible.

Beside Stoker, several first editions by Sheridan Le Fanu including *In a Glass Darkly* (1872). I had heard of the prominent Irish Gothicist Le Fanu and knew of his great influence on Bram Stoker's *Dracula,* but I had never read a word he'd written.

To my chagrin I was discovering that the Haider library contained earlier, far more valuable first edition copies of books which I'd proudly acquired for my library—a signed first edition of Henry James's *The Turn of the Screw* (1899), where I had only a first, unsigned edition; a signed first edition of Algernon

Blackwood's *The Empty House* (1906), where I had only an un-signed second edition; signed first editions of Wilkie Collins's *The Moonstone, The Woman in White, No Name*—where I had only unsigned, later editions. And there was Edgar Allan Poe's *The Imp of the Perverse* in a slender, much-worn volume, dated 1846—one of that troubled genius's later, little-known works of fiction in the guise of memoir; or, was *The Imp of the Perverse* memoir in the guise of fiction? How paltry the acquisitions of Andrew J. Rush were, set beside the Haider collection. (Yet more shamefully, I have to confess that I'd read less than one-tenth of my library, in fact. I had done my voracious reading as an adolescent and as a young writer in my twenties. In later years it has become the *possessing/displaying* of books that mattered to me, and not the actual reading of any book however masterly.)

Elsewhere on the shelves, of lesser interest to me, were leather-bound sets of the old, dutiful English classics—*Collected Works of Shakespeare, Milton, Thackeray, Dickens, Sir Walter Scott.* Volumes of verse by Byron, Wordsworth, Tennyson, Hardy, Matthew Arnold. Still, there were oddities—a dozen books by a writer of whom I had never heard, Ivy Compton-Burnett; at least a dozen by Iris Murdoch of whom I'd certainly heard, but had never read.

Of course, I told myself that the Haider family was a very old New Jersey family, dating back to pre-Revolutionary times; one of the Haider ancestors had been an aide of General George Washington, another a governor of New Jersey in the early 1900s. As C. W. Haider had inherited this property in a still-distinguished neighborhood in Harbourton, so she had inherited these precious books. Perhaps her father or her grandfather had been a serious collector. No credit was due to *her*.

Seeing the caretaker through a window, earnestly raking in the overgrown backyard, I slipped several of the rare books into my duffel bag—volumes I and II of *Frankenstein, The Lair of the White Worm, The Turn of the Screw;* cleverly, I rearranged the books so that there were no gaping absences on the shelves.

She doesn't deserve these books! She has not glanced into them in years.

To the victor, the spoils.

By this time the silky black cat had jumped down from its perch on the sofa, to approach me with a hoarse, somehow jeering *yyyow*—still swishing his tail, and still glaring with its eyes like gold coins.

"Nice kitty! Are you—'Satan'?"

I laughed, for the name had come to me out of nowhere.

"'Satan'? Are you? Kitty-kitty?"—I stooped to pet the cat, for it was very beautiful and seemed to be inviting me; but it miao'd angrily, bristled its silky back like a Hallowe'en cat, and bared its teeth in a way that did not seem welcoming.

"Go to hell, then—'Satan.' Where you belong."

The rebuff by Haider's cat was hurtful for animals are always fond of me—dogs especially. Cats of course are notoriously less predictable, despite their beauty.

As I explored the room more thoroughly, I saw that it opened into a kitchen (high-ceiling, old-fashioned fixtures) at one end, and a drawing room (shrouded furniture, dank odor) at the other. The degree of clutter here suggested hoarding, or rather the onset of hoarding: stacks of aged newspapers, magazines, advertising circulars and brochures. A singular stack rising from the floor, like a stalagmite, of old books including what appeared to be books from the Harbourton Public Library, long overdue. One day soon, the interior of the dignified old Edwardian house might be near-impassable. Narrow nightmare passageways for the madwoman to make her way through . . .

Near the fireplace was what must have been Haider's favorite place for sitting, a once-elegant Victorian chair covered in a cobwebby sort of velvet, with sagging seat like sagging buttocks; beside the chair was a table stacked with (surprisingly) recently published hardcover books of which not one but two were by Stephen King; I saw to my alarm that one was my 2004 novel *Outside, In.* (Had Haider been sifting through the sentences of this elaborately plotted mystery to see if she could discover "sources"—"influence"? I did not dare to take up the book, to leaf through it and see her notes. Best not to know.)

What can the witch prove! She is insane, discredited.

An injunction has been served against her *to protect* you.

The fireplace was as large as the fireplace at Mill Brook House of which I was so proud, comprised of the same sort of fieldstone and stucco. This fireplace was filled with ashes, however—unlike ours, which was kept clean by the young Guatemalan girls who came on Mondays to clean our house. Brass andirons here badly needed polishing. Firewood was stacked on the hearth carelessly, as if it had been thrown down; an ax lay on the hearth, also looking as if it had been flung down. The ax was of another era, with a crude head and weathered wooden handle; its edge could not have been very sharp, yet someone (Esdra? Haider herself?) had been gamely trying to split small logs with it, causing a good deal of splintering. There was a pile of kindling also, covered in cobwebs, and some old, badly discolored newspapers on the floor. By the newspaper's fussy font I recognized the *Harbourton Weekly*.

In the gritty film of ashes on the floor, near the fireplace hearth, were myriad paw prints. You'd have thought there had been a witch's Sabbath here—so many paw prints! But all were Satan's, surely.

The kitchen floor was covered in linoleum tile, unpleasantly sticky beneath my feet. The gas stove was very old, and its burners rusted; the refrigerator was a General Electric, that must have dated from the 1970s, and gave off a dull, guttural sound as of indigestion. On woven place mats on the kitchen floor—place mats that must have been fairly expensive—were at least five cat dishes, containing food and water; it seemed clear that Esdra kept his mistress's black cat well-fed and watered. And in the rear kitchen door was a small, swinging plastic door, which had to be the cat's. The spoiled creature could exit and enter the house at will, it seemed.

Why was I thinking suddenly of Edgar Allan Poe's "The Black Cat"—the creature that is beloved by his master, yet for no clear reason strangled to death by his master and shut up inside a wall; and out of that wall issues the (dead) animal's bloodcurdling caterwaul, to drive the master insane . . .

"That won't happen to me."

(Why did I say this aloud? In fact, did I say it aloud? Sometimes I am not sure if I have spoken to myself, or only just thought something. Or, if someone else has spoken to me.)

Haider's kitchen had probably not been renovated for decades. There was an aroma here of rancid food, spoiled milk and rotted fruit; grime, dust, sorrow. Yet, the aroma was not altogether unpleasant, like the smell of an old blanket that has been on your bed for years and has been rarely laundered.

Here too, you could see that the wild-white-haired Haider had a favorite chair at the plank-topped table. Of several chairs, just one had a (grimy) cushion, and faced, on a counter, a television set so small it looked at first like a toy. Overhead, a ninety-watt lightbulb hung down on a chain, unadorned. I felt a pang of pity for the lonely spinster—Haider must have eaten her solitary meals here, and tried to read, or watched TV.

I had the idea that it was Haider who was estranged from her relatives, and not the reverse. Younger relatives would have imagined that the elderly woman would one day leave them something in her will. Still, I felt sorry for her.

It is not your fault that the woman is the enemy.

It is not your fault, the woman tried to publicly destroy Andrew J. Rush.

This was true! I could not forget this.

I returned to the other room and took from a bookshelf one of the dingy old volumes by Le Fanu to slip into my duffel bag. Also, a copy of H. G. Wells's *The Island of Dr. Moreau*, which I had not noticed before, and which was surely a collector's item like the others. And—for I'd been unable to resist, the slender volume *The Imp of the Perverse.* Outside the window, oblivious of such blatant theft, the faithful caretaker was raking debris into piles.

She will never miss any of these. She is rich, careless—she does not deserve such treasures.

After I'd set the tinsel-wrapped box onto Haider's desk I'd stepped quickly away, and had avoided that part of the room. I was fearful that the wild-white-haired woman's aura emanated from the desk—frustration, failure, fury, madness—and to breathe in this aura might infect me.

Prominent on the desk was an old-fashioned Remington typewriter, a heavy office model; placed about the typewriter were neatly typed manuscript pages. (Out of a terror of being infected I did not want to glance down to see the title of any manuscript of C. W. Haider.) On a high shelf above the window, running along the length of the wall, arranged chronologically, were Haider's journals—dreadful to see, so many journals, from the 1960s through the decades, diligently, doggedly, to the present time—2014. Even if I could have reached up easily to seize one of these journals I had no wish to glance into it. In a small bookcase beside the table were C. W. Haider's own works. The very oldest, dating to the 1960s, were school publications in which poetry and prose by "Corin Wren Haider" appeared. (So that was the name of my nemesis! "Corin Wren"—a name to evoke pitying smiles among classmates.) There were self-published books, some of them lavishly designed, with *C. W. Haider* on the spines. The first, presumably the oldest, was titled *Haider & Haider: A Potpourri of Verse*—a joint authorship of W. J. Haider & C. W. Haider—father, daughter? The publication date was 1973.

Out of curiosity I stooped to scan other titles in the bookshelf—one, in gilt lettering, was *Criss-Cross*!

This was a stunning discovery, like a blow to the heart.

How was it possible that C. W. Haider had written a seventy-page novella titled *Criss-Cross,* published by a vanity press in 1999—the very title of my novel-in-progress, which had been giving me such trouble for the past several months . . .

Had Haider "donated" copies of her books to the Harbourton library? Was it likely that, altogether innocently, I'd happened to see the intriguing title on a bookshelf there one day, of which I had no memory?

Truly, I didn't think so.

I had thought *Criss-Cross* was an ideal title for my novel, which was to be one of my strongest, most ingenious novels. An inspired title I had not chosen easily. And I could not change it now, for the plot's structure reflected the title, and vice versa.

Andrew J. Rush, known as the gentleman's Stephen King, has created an unusually clever and original plot for his twenty-ninth novel . . .

In an intriguing stylistic departure from his previous work, Andrew J. Rush, the "gentleman's Stephen King," has surprised us with . . .

So I had fantasized early reviews.

Possibly even my first full review in the *New York Times*.

(Shamelessly, I'd even fantasized that Stephen King might review *Criss-Cross* on the coveted front page of the *New York Times Book Review*. But now I seemed to know that would never occur.)

Now, *Criss-Cross* seemed to jeer at me. But after months of labor I could not imagine changing the title . . .

C. W. Haider would be furious when she saw that I had "stolen" this title. Despite the injunction, she might pursue me again. I hoped it would not provoke the madwoman to anything desperate.

So far as I knew, Haider had never come out to Mill Brook House. She had yet to "stalk" me as Elliot Grossman had predicted she might.

If she enters your residence to threaten you, you have the right to kill her.

If she has cast a curse onto your life, you have every right to defend yourself.

By this time I was sitting in Haider's writing chair, for my knees had grown weak. This was a straight-backed dining room chair with a soiled chintz cushion. I made no effort to see what new project Haider was working on—(I dreaded being "influenced" as I would dread being exposed to Ebola)—but I could not resist scanning the brave little library of self-published books by C. W. Haider—there had to be at least as many as my own books, which were published by an "authentic" publisher.

Here was another novella-length book with an intriguing title—*The Glowering* (1974).

Out of curiosity I skimmed the first chapter. And then the second, and the third . . . Hairs stirred on the nape of my neck for the story depicted an idealistic young woman mystery writer named "Corrin Wingate" who (naïvely) accepts a position as caretaker of a remote luxury hotel in the Adirondacks at Styxl Lake, purportedly north of Saranac Lake, during the off-season when the hotel is snowbound. The young woman is not only a "gifted" writer but has the gift of "the Glowering"— i.e., "second sight." (She can see into the future, though not clearly; she can have no power over changing the future.) The young woman writer takes a cousin-companion with her to Styxl Lake, and each of the young women brings her pet cat; soon after their arrival at the majestic Hotel Styxl they are beset by hallucinatory/demonic presences, soon, the young woman writer is unable to write, and she and her cousin-companion begin to succumb to paranoid fantasies . . . Though written in an annoyingly florid style, quaintly "poetic" in the worst meaning of that word, *The Glowering* told a gripping story of disintegration in the wilderness; though the chapters were overlong and absurdly melodramatic, each chapter was a self-enclosed scene, passionately rendered. A scene in which the writer's pet cat becomes infected by a demon and turns first against the other cat and then against its mistress was particularly spellbinding—and terrifying.

The Glowering had been published several years before Stephen King's *The Shining* (which I knew to be 1977—I'd been impressed, as a young writer.) How strange!

Could it be, the young Stephen King had in some way appropriated C. W. Haider's unknown *The Glowering?* It was impossible to believe, and yet . . .

Another novella by C. W. Haider in the bookcase was titled *The Shadow Self.* This ninety-page work of fiction hadn't been published, apparently; the typed manuscript was bound in marbled boards and dated (in ink) February 1983. A quick skimming of its (overwrought, "poetic") pages suggested that this was a Gothic tale of an idealistic young woman mystery writer ("Carroll Wheeler") who has been overtaken by her (male) pseudonym, or alter ego: the (male) writer publishes novels of "sickening, lewd horror" while the (female) writer publishes "well-received literary fiction"; the (male) writer begins to achieve commercial success, while the (female) writer achieves only critical acclaim, and a scattering of prizes. In an effort to exorcise the (male) writer, the (female) writer burns his books and sweeps the ashes into a swampy pit; after only a few days of "refreshing, joyous freedom from the shackles of evil" the (female) writer is overwhelmed by the (male) writer who has somehow (not clear how) managed to murder half the population of the "historic" New Jersey village that is the novella's setting. An absurdly melodramatic horror story which (I must confess) I couldn't finish though its plot was certainly familiar to me—in outline, very similar to Stephen King's *The Dark Half* which had to have been written years after C. W. Haider's *The Shadow Self.*

Again, it was preposterous to think that Stephen King had somehow had access to Haider's (unpublished) novella. Even if the desperate would-be writer had sent the manuscript to him, King wouldn't have glanced into it; if he'd glanced into it, King wouldn't have read more than a paragraph or two, for the prose was typically overwrought and "elevated."

Carefully, I put *The Shadow Self* back on the shelf. I did not want to think—(I was not going to think)—of my own increasingly uneasy relationship with Jack of Spades.

On another shelf was a similarly bound manuscript, C. W. Haider's *Sister Witches of Hecate County* (1979), which would seem to have predated John Updike's *The Witches of Eastwick.* (I recalled that Grossman had told me laughingly that Haider had tried to sue Updike.) And there was Haider's *Ghost-Tales of the Chilliwick Club* (1974), a lengthy novel with a complicated chronology and numerous characters which must have predated Peter Straub's notably complicated *Ghost Story* by several years.

Coincidence? Had to be.

Could not be.

Here was a shock! On the lower-most bookshelf, a ravaged copy of my novel of 1991, *Murder at Midnight.* This had been one of those novels of mine that my publisher had hoped would be a "breakout" publication to propel Andrew J. Rush to the very top of the bestseller list; unfortunately this did not happen, though the novel lingered on the lower rungs of the list for several weeks, and sold well in paperback. It was distressing to discover that Haider had gone through the book with a red pen luridly annotating virtually every paragraph . . . This wholly original mystery of formerly conjoined twins, each believing the other had died after their surgical separation, I will swear was entirely my own; yet Haider seemed to have typed a thirty-page outline of a near-identical plot of a novel titled *Murder at Dusk* which she'd sent, with a "sample first chapter," to a New York publishing house in April 1987—receiving back a form rejection slip.

Yet more distressing, the New York publishing house was my own.

The parallels between *Murder at Midnight* and *Murder at Dusk* were undeniable. In the last chapter of each, a "good" twin had triumphed over an "evil" twin—unless it was the reverse.

I didn't doubt that Haider had imagined this mystery story in 1987, years before I'd even begun writing my novel. But *I had not* stolen from it!

No doubt Haider had read from *Murder at Midnight* and from *Murder at Dusk* in the courtroom, in her mocking voice. Out of mortification I had tried not to listen. Now a wave of shame swept over me, that Andrew J. Rush had been publicly shamed after all.

In a drawer in Haider's writing table was a bulging manila file containing letters from this publisher as well as other New York publishers, and from magazines (*Saturday Evening Post, The New Yorker, The Atlantic*) dating from the early 1970s. Most of the letters were brief, succinct paragraphs of form rejections—*We are sorry to inform you* . . . A few were personalized, and one, from a (female) editor at St. Martin's Press, in 2003, included a handwritten postscript—*This almost worked for me! Please send more.*

How hopeful Haider must have felt, receiving this letter! But it appeared to be the only one of its kind amid the deluge of formula rejections.

There was another, deep drawer filled with manila folders—typed pages, outlines, sketches; line-drawings, family photos, newspaper clippings. The dank-toadstool odor of abject failure wafted from this drawer, leaving me faint. Desperately I slammed the drawer shut.

I was feeling dazed, exhausted. I had not eaten since an early lunch, for my dear wife Irina had abandoned me for dinner, preferring to have her evening meal with her "colleagues"—including the lanky jet-black-haired "Huang Lee."

A furry shape pushed against my legs with mock affection—the silky black Satan, nudging with his hard head. The cat's loud purring seemed a kind of crude cat laughter.

"But—I am innocent. Truly I did not 'steal' . . . plagiarize' . . ."

It was the black cat which I had to convince. The black cat staring at me with bemused eyes.

I could not comprehend what I'd discovered—whether the eerily close parallels between Haider's work and the work of her successful contemporaries were simply coincidental, or could not possibly be coincidental.

"Poor woman! Always to have missed . . ."

From a young age Haider had tried to be a writer; she'd had inspired ideas, brilliant ideas for mystery-horror novels, but had been (evidently) incapable of executing these ideas as others had, with enormous commercial success. Was *Murder at Dusk* really so inferior to *Murder at Midnight?*—I didn't want to read the sample first chapter, to see.

Scattered about the writer's room were family photographs. It seemed clear that, even when she was young, C. W. Haider had not been an attractive person. As a child she'd virtually sneered at the camera. Her features were hawkish, peevish; even sitting for a formal photograph, she didn't deign to smile. In a glaring-white graduation cap and gown (high school? college?) the aggressively homely girl stood stiff and unyielding with a look of pride; you could see that her faith in herself was fierce though (as it turned out) unfounded. In her early thirties she had certainly resembled Ayn Rand. Of course it had not helped Haider's career that she was *female*, but *not feminine*. She'd hoped to break into a male-dominated field of popular American mystery-horror writing as few women have been able to do, and certainly not a woman writer who displayed the ego of a male writer.

Perhaps if Haider been more attractive, or in some way more *feminine*, she might have convinced an editor to read her work seriously, and to help her revise it for publication. But that was not to be. No wonder the poor woman had gone mad.

Don't be softheaded. She hates you.

Recall: you have immunity in this house.

This was so. As Jack of Spades had perceived, I had a kind of immunity in this house in Tumbrel Place. Judge Carson (indeed, a friendly acquaintance of mine who might have recused himself from the case, but had not) had ruled, C. W. Haider's case against Andrew J. Rush had been dismissed, and dismissed with obvious contempt. If she accused me of "stealing" from her ever again, she would be laughed out of court.

Would Harbourton police listen to her? I doubted it.

I had prevailed upon Elliot Grossman not to sue Haider but I had relented and allowed him to file for an injunction against her to prevent further harassment.

Grossman had joked, "With this injunction, the old witch can't harass you. But you could, if you were a vindictive person, harass *her*."

I hadn't laughed. I told Grossman that wasn't funny.

"Hey, I'm sorry, Andrew. Just a joke."

"It isn't funny. I've told you, the poor woman is mentally ill. Why would I want to 'harass' someone who is mentally ill?"

I was so angry at Grossman, it was all I could do to stop from grinding my back teeth. Fortunately we were speaking on the phone and Grossman couldn't see the expression on my face, which felt savage.

Now, the conversation returned to me. *You could, if you were a vindictive person, harass* her.

Well, I did not want to harass C. W. Haider. It was punishment enough for the overbearing woman that she was a total failure as a writer; that she'd had to be committed for psychiatric examination; and that she'd lost her case against me.

I didn't consider that removing a few of the precious rare books in Haider's library constituted "harassment" of any kind. My reasoning was that Haider would (probably) never notice the books were missing. Nor did I consider my acquisition of the books "theft"—for the same reason.

She owes you. You didn't sue for legal fees.

I decided to take a copy of Haider's self-published *The Glowering*. She would certainly never miss this since she had a half-dozen copies on the shelf, and what a collector's item it was in its own bizarre way.

Not that I would keep this curious novella on one of the open shelves in my house. I would keep it in my special storage area in the basement with *Jack of Spades*.

Before I left the house I looked for the security alarm. I know where such things are installed, usually in a closet; I intended to dismantle it, but saw that it was already dismantled. The Edwardian house at 88 Tumbrel Place had no security beyond locks on its doors and windows.

In one of the shut-off rooms, I unlocked a corner window that Esdra would never notice. As a precaution, I unlocked a second window, in a parlor.

In case I wanted to revisit the Haider residence—though certainly I had no intention of revisiting "the scene of the crime."

As I was about to leave I rapped on a window to indicate to Esdra that I was departing. The caretaker, still raking debris, smiled at me and touched his fingers to his forehead in a kind of salute. It was a gesture of camaraderie—the black servant and the white gentleman-visitor bonded in our wish to protect the beleaguered C. W. Haider.

* * *

Though I should have been excited by my new collector's items I found myself feeling curiously deflated, anticlimactic, on my drive home.

I'd removed my old glasses. I'd tossed away the grimy baseball cap. As I turned into the driveway and approached Mill Brook House I saw that Irina's car was still gone though it had seemed to me I'd been away from home for a very long time.

17   The Secret Library

Days, weeks. Waiting.

At first, I eagerly checked local news for reports of a burglary at the Haider house. Or any news of C. W. Haider.

Had Haider been discharged from the hospital? Had she returned home? How had she reacted to the "gift" on her writing table, insolently signed *Steve King*?

Maybe she'd been so insulted by this prank, she'd had a relapse. A second breakdown.

I believed that, if Haider had died, there'd have been a prominent obituary in the *Harbourton Weekly*. But there was no obituary.

Once, I dared to drive past 88 Tumbrel Place. I felt a powerful attraction to the gaunt, ugly Edwardian house with its aged bricks and storm-damaged trees. I hoped for a glimpse of the faithful caretaker at least, but I saw no one. And no one at any of the tall narrow windows facing the street.

Don't go inside now. You would be risking too much.

As if I needed Jack of Spades to caution me.

* * *

"Esdra? Hello . . ."

At the Harbourton Mall, in the parking lot behind Macy's there came at a brisk pace a short squat blunt-headed black man in work clothes, and the sight of him so excited me, though I could see (certainly, I could see) that this man was much younger than Esdra Staples, I braked my car to a stop, and leaned out the window to call to him; but the man was a stranger, his eyes on me were startled, wary.

"Sorry, sir! Mistook you for an old friend."

Damn.

Out of caution, I had to hide my precious new acquisitions in the converted fruit cellar, in the special storage space where Jack of Spades resided in the basement of Mill Brook House. Though none of the books was identified as having belonged to Haider—nothing so vulgar as a book plate in a rare book, certainly!—I could not—yet—risk keeping my extraordinary signed books—*Frankenstein, The Lair of the White Worm, The Turn of the Screw, In a Glass Darkly, The Island of Dr. Moreau*— and the unique *Imp of the Perverse*—amid my upstairs collection where they might be perused by admiring visitors, though there was nothing I'd have liked better.

Yet you left Dracula *behind. Fool.*

This did nag at me. Why hadn't I slipped the signed *Dracula* into my duffel bag when I'd had the opportunity? If Haider failed to notice the other missing books, she wouldn't notice the absence of *Dracula* either.

The converted fruit cellar was a windowless room—of course. I'd painted it myself: beige walls, white ceiling. Though the ceiling was low at about six feet, scarcely two inches above my head, the space was oddly comforting, as it was snug and secret. Each wall was comprised of bookshelves but partly filled; for Jack of Spades was still in the ascendency of his career. I would leave shelves empty, to be filled in time. But the new, rare books were prominently placed at eye level, on a shelf of their own.

Now that valuable rare books were to be kept in the secret library (as I'd come to think of the room) I'd installed a dehumidifier, as I had a dehumidifier upstairs. (I'd discovered that the *Frankenstein* volumes alone were worth more than seventy-five thousand dollars!) It was my reasoning that if/when something happened to C. W. Haider, and there was no possibility of the books being traced to her, I would bring them upstairs to be proudly displayed.

When I entered the secret library I could lock the door behind me, and feel utterly safe. Even when the children were still living in this house they'd rarely taken any interest in their father's book-collecting just as (I'm sorry to say) they'd rarely taken much interest in their father's writing career.

Once, in fifth grade, our older son, Chris, had come home from school (at that time in Highland Park) to ask Irina— "Does Dad write 'middle-brow mysteries'?" We'd laughed together at the question, and the prejudice behind it, but in truth, I had not thought it was funny. (Never mind what sly, circuitous revenge I'd enacted upon the unsuspecting snob of a fifth-grade teacher, who'd soon had to send his résumé out upon shark-infested waters, in search of another teaching job. Smug bastard!)

Julia had read several mysteries by her daddy, in high school. She'd claimed to find them "real page-turners" and "filled with surprises" but (I happened to know) she'd ceased reading my books as an undergraduate at Brown, and seemed mildly embarrassed when anyone asked her if her father was *the* Andrew J. Rush. ("You should be proud of your father, Julia!" Irina chided her; and Julia said, "Well, I am, Mom—I just feel kind of self-conscious when people ask me because I don't actually know what they think about Dad.")

As for the boys—Chris wasn't much of a reader of fiction, by his own admission; and Dale, by his own admission, wasn't much of a reader of anything. Both were "in computers"— medium-range jobs in medium-range companies in New Jersey. In their mid-twenties both our sons played video games for "relaxation."

So far as I knew, Irina read everything by Andrew J. Rush. Her reactions were always highly positive. What had become of the sharp-eyed, astute critic of our fiction workshop of years ago? Had my dear wife adjusted her critical expectations downward, to a comfort-level appropriate to Andrew J. Rush? Was my dear wife *condescending*?

JACK OF SPADES

None of them knew anything about Jack of Spades. I smiled to think how shocked my family would be, if they knew.

Yes but they won't. That is our secret.

Jack of Spades seemed new in my life, and so it was a surprising fact that a fifth novel by Jack of Spades was due to appear in a few weeks, in October. Utter secrecy would surround this publication, though the publisher planned some minimal advertisements, or had vaguely promised some advertisements. The new novel was *Scourge,* which I'd written in such a protracted siege of concentration the previous winter, I could barely recall the plot now; where each sentence by Andrew J. Rush was an effort, and felt at times as if I were dragging mangled veins and arteries out of my body to impress upon a blank page, entire passages and pages, even chapters, by "Jack of Spades" passed in a rabid blur leaving me exhausted, but gratified. My recollection of *Scourge* was that it had an abrupt, ugly ending, an unexpected murder-suicide in some murky waters, below a steep precipice; as usual, the Jack of Spades protagonist was confronted by a mocking Doppelganger who threatened his wife, his family, and himself, and had to be dispatched by violence.

Bound galleys of *Scourge,* sent to my post office box in Hadrian, were on a shelf here, adjacent to paperbacks by Jack of Spades. Out of curiosity I checked the cover, which I'd forgotten—it was something of a shock, to see that the cover art for *Scourge* crudely replicated a familiar Gustav Klimt erotic portrait of a

143

sexually voracious woman. (Had I given permission for this? Evidently!) In the original Klimt the nude female had vivid red hair springing from her head while on the book cover the nude female had snowy-white hair though there was no mistaking her avid sexuality. In both, the nude female was lying in a suggestive pose, hands behind her head and arms spread to expose patches of underarm hair.

Sick. Macho-male.

Novels to make you think—but not nice thoughts.

I wondered if Julia had read more novels by Jack of Spades. It was irritating to me, that my daughter was so headstrong, and so stubbornly *feminist*. I hated to think of her as a "mature" young woman living her own, inscrutable life—hated to think of her as sexually involved with anyone . . .

"Hello? Andrew?"—a voice behind me, unexpectedly.

It was Irina. I'd left the door to the secret library ajar, and Irina was standing just outside.

"Why, what is this? A kind of—underground library?"

Until now, Irina hadn't seen the "storage room"—though I'd told her that I was using the space for surplus books. Her widened eyes suggested how surprised she was, seeing the built-in shelves, the recessed lighting, a single black leather easy chair, even a rug on the floor.

Quickly I pushed Irina back, stepped outside, and shut the door.

"Darling, are you spying on me? I hope not."

" 'Spying'—? No, I—I thought I'd heard . . ."

"Let's go upstairs, please. I was just leaving."

Trying to smile at my dear wife. Trying not to sound brusque, annoyed.

She knows too much. Simply knowing there is a place in this house secret from her is knowing too much.

It was annoying to me too, that Irina was wearing makeup—pale coral lipstick, a glaze of powder—and a silver necklace, and silver bracelet—signaling she'd been at the Friends School that day, among her colleagues. She was dressed nicely, and had done something to her hair. On her feet were striking shoes, open-backed sandals with a small heel, I was sure I'd never seen before. At home, with just husband Andrew, Irina rarely troubled with makeup, wore jeans and shapeless shirts and sweaters and an old pair of running shoes.

It was late September. Several months since the day of the summons.

Since *the enemy* had intruded in my life.

"Andrew, why do you seem so—angry? I'm sorry if I disturbed you—I wasn't 'spying' on you—truly . . . I'd just come home and thought I'd say hello—you weren't in your study—I thought I heard voices in the basement . . ."

" 'Voices'? Don't be absurd."

"Well, I—I guess I was mistaken. I'm sorry."

"How could there have been *voices*? There is no one here except me."

We were upstairs now. Irina was shrinking from me. Stammering apologetically she said she'd thought there might have been someone with me, a repairman, a delivery man—"I'm so sorry, I'm mistaken. Why is it so important? Why are you so *angry?*"

Seeing fear in the woman's eyes. *Why the hell is a wife of mine frightened—of me?*

"I am not angry, Irina! That's an insult."

Still Irina shrank from me, and would have hurried away except my hand leapt out to seize her shoulder—she gave a little cry of surprise and pain—and at once I released her.

For a moment we stared at each other, both of us shocked, and panting. I could not believe that my wife had provoked me to behave in a way totally contrary to my nature, nor that she would exacerbate the situation by saying, half-sobbing, "I hate it when you drink, Andrew. You're not yourself—you frighten me."

"*That's* an insult. I haven't been drinking."

Irina ran from me, upstairs. Damned if I would follow her.

She is jealous of you. Your talent, your success.

That you are a man, and superior to her. That alone, the woman can't bear.

Later, I returned to the secret library.

Wanting to check the lock on the door. Wanting to check the dehumidifier. Wanting to admire the new acquisitions of which I was so strangely *proud*—as if I'd salvaged these rare books from Hell itself.

The house was darkened. Irina had gone to bed. I imagined her eyes swollen from weeping. Damned if I would seek her out another time.

Too often lately, these inexplicable scenes sprang up between us. As if Irina were daring to provoke me, to see how far she could push her good-natured husband before he'd snap.

Her behavior had something to do with the fall term at the Friends School. As if her emotional center of gravity had shifted and was no longer in this house, but *there*.

And not you, the husband. But him.

I'd had just a glimpse of the man "Thiang Tai." W'(ll lu i n driving on a road just outside Harbourton and Irina had waved out the window of the station wagon at a bicyclist—male, jet-black-haired, in tight blue spandex shorts and T shirt whom I'd assumed to be a student at the Friends School until Irina identified him as a math teacher colleague.

When he recognized Irina, he'd waved in reply.

My vehicle sped past missing him by a wide margin.

Since that time I realized: often over the past several months I'd been hearing Irina on her cell phone, in odd parts of the house. Or outdoors, a distance from the house. As if she were hiding from me—from *me*, the husband.

And it seemed too that Irina was going out of her way to provoke me. As if she were tempting me to anger. Tempting me to lay a hand on her.

I am not the sort of man who eavesdrops on his wife, or on anyone. I am not the sort of man who lays a hand on his wife, or on anyone.

In the secret library, taking care to shut and lock the door behind me. Splashing an inch or two of Scotch whiskey into a glass, out of a bottle kept here for such a purpose.

She knows nothing of you.

None of them do.

Recalling Edgar Allan Poe's story "The Black Cat" in which the wife is strangled as well as the pet cat, and both are sealed up in a wall out of which a terrible wailing rises.

18   The Repentant

Take care! You are in great danger.

For a night and a part of the next day Irina avoided me. In my writing room above the old stable I was unable to work. Sick in the gut, and sick at heart. The very thought of Jack of Spades filled me with dismay.

"I will have to stop. No more 'Jack of Spades.'"

I waited, apprehensive. As one who has felt a tinge in his heart waits for a greater tinge, and cardiac catastrophe.

Waited for the jeering threatening voice.

And yet—there was nothing. Outside the opened windows a soughing of wind in the tall trees that surrounded the house, a beautiful sound that brought tears to my eyes.

"I will give back the books I've taken from that poor woman. I will apologize to Irina. I will never drink again."

Early that morning before I was fully awake Irina had left for the Friends School. For the first time in our marriage one of us had left the house without saying good-bye to the other.

It was a small thing, I knew. It was a chasm.

I'd fallen into a stuporous sleep in the basement room the previous night. The empty bottle of Scotch at my feet.

When I came upstairs groggy and uncertain at nearly 9:00 A.M. my wife was gone, the house was empty and in all the rooms a sharp white autumn sun shone through the windows, meaninglessly—a premonition of Mill Brook House empty of its inhabitants.

"Irina? Where are you . . ."

My head ached. Pulses in my eyes pounded with ominous intent. As if someone, some thing, were trying to speak to me.

That day, which was an interminable day, I could not write a coherent sentence. In my writing room that had been the setting of more than one admiring feature in local publications—("airy"—"spacious"—"gorgeous rural views"—"private, secluded"—"a writer's dream")—I'd been unable to concentrate. How mechanical, the plot of *Criss-Cross*! And how hollow-sounding, the title of which I'd been so proud. Sentences careened through my brain like deranged beetles. Words became detached from their meanings. When I tried to read aloud passages that needed particular attention—which I have always done—it was the jeering voice of the wild-white-haired woman that rang in my ears.

Thief! Plagiarist! Murderer!

"I am not a—murderer . . ."

In your heart, you are a murderer. You want your enemy dead.

"I don't want anyone dead. I—I am terrified of hurting another person . . ."

You are terrified only of being exposed of your crimes, and punished. That is all.

"This is not true! In my heart, I am not that way at all."

Ugly din of voices. C. W. Haider, Jack of Spades. In my confusion I could not tell them apart.

There was a marshy area on our property, in a low-lying field not far from Mill Brook, that smelled strongly of rot, manure. Very likely it was a cesspool into which animal waste had once drained from the barnyard. Irina and I had discovered the "marsh"—as we (euphemistically) called it—and had thought we might have the area filled in with topsoil. But we'd never gotten around to ordering the topsoil. Even in high boots you wouldn't want to walk in the "marsh" you would fear being sucked into the soft mucky earth. And the stench of rot, organic decay. And the clouds of gnats, flies, butterflies that hovered above the marsh, a terrifying teeming of life.

Nonetheless there were beautiful creatures in the marsh. Butterflies of many sizes and colors. Red-winged blackbirds, snowy egrets.

Copperhead snakes, snapping like miniature whips.

Jack of Spades was the soft sinking treacherous marsh. You could dump solid topsoil into it—but the topsoil would be sucked down. You could lay planks across the marsh—but the planks would be sucked down.

Best to avoid the marsh. The poisonous fumes were intoxicating, addictive.

* * *

"Irina? I'm so sorry. I don't know what came over me . . . I hadn't realized I'd been drinking so much. I hadn't realized I'd been drinking *at all*."

Taking Irina's small-boned hands in my hands. Stroking her fingers that were stiff in my fingers, not quite resisting, yet not yielding.

It was so: I had no clear idea what had come over me the previous night. Why I'd been so suddenly furious with my dear wife whom I loved very much—whom I adore.

"Do you forgive me, Irina? I swear it won't happen again."

Irina's eyes were downcast. Her manner was subdued, wary.

"It's this strain I've been under, that I haven't wanted to tell you about . . ."

This caused Irina to glance up at me, as I'd hoped it would.

". . . I've been shielding from you since it's both very petty and very destructive."

"What is it?"

"Just something to do with my writing—my 'career.' The vicissitudes of Andrew J. Rush."

"But 'Andrew J. Rush' *is you*. Please tell me what has happened . . ."

I felt a pang of love for my wife of so many years. Dear Irina who'd fallen in love with "Andy Rush" who was so much her inferior, hadn't she known?

These many years, I'd managed to deceive her.

My career, not *hers*. Why hadn't Irina Kacizk struggled more assertively, why had she subordinated herself to *me*?

Irina had been gone all that day—from approximately 8:00
A.M. until 6:00 P.M.—and hadn't answered her cell phone despite my numerous calls. Of course, I had hurt her feelings. A
woman too has pride, and must not allow herself to seem over-submissive in a marriage. Yet my dear Irina was so devoted to
me, and her livelihood so bound up with *Andrew J. Rush*, she'd
become unhesitatingly sympathetic.

"Darling, do you know the name 'Haider'?"

"'Hater'—what a strange name!"

"Not 'Hater'—'Haider.' They're a local family."

Irina frowned, and thought a moment. "Well, yes—
'Haider'—that name is familiar. They've made contributions
in Harbourton—there's a park named for them, and a schol
arship fund at the Friends School. I think there's a student in
the school right now in the upper form. But no one I know."

In a sudden rush of words I confessed: an older woman named
Haider, a resident of Harbourton, and a failed, would-be writer,
had attempted to sue Andrew J. Rush early in the summer. But
the suit had been dismissed.

Irina waited for me to continue. "And—?"

"And—that's all. She'd initiated a lawsuit on some ridiculous
claim of invasion of privacy, but the case was thrown out of
court."

Invasion of privacy was more plausible than *theft, plagiarism,*
as it was less painful.

"'Invasion of privacy'—how absurd. How could she make
such a claim?"

"It was a typical nuisance suit, my publisher's lawyer told me. The sort of thing that happens often to successful high-profile writers usually, like Stephen King."

"But you are 'successful' and 'high-profile' also, Andrew! I'm so sorry that this upset you, and you hadn't even told me about it. I can understand why you've been distracted."

"Even more outrageous, she tried to sue me for 'stealing'— 'plagiarizing'—from *her*."

"My God! What a joke."

Irina's warm brown eyes filled with tears of angry commiseration. She had many wifely questions to ask but I assured her that there was nothing more to be said—really. "The lawsuit was considered groundless, and the case was dismissed by Judge Carson."

Now Irina took my hands in hers, to quell their tremor.

"But why are you so agitated, Andrew? If it has been dismissed?"

19   Tumbrel Place II

No one will know! You will be spotless as a lamb.

Another time, I drove to Tumbrel Place, Harbourton. Except this time, it was after midnight.

Dark as a tar pit, the old "historic" neighborhood near the courthouse.

And now, it was well into autumn, the first week of November, and the nights frankly cold. Very sensible of anyone who ventured out after midnight to wear gloves, leather jacket, a fedora pulled low over his forehead.

All of my clothes were dark-hued. And my Nike running shoes, black.

Irina had no idea where I was. No idea I'd gone out. I'd waited until my dear wife had gone to bed, and was soundly asleep well before midnight. And then I'd slipped away from the house unobserved.

Overhead, a faint red moon. Some rogue impulse inspired me to smile at the moon, and wink.

Only you, my witness.
And you will never tell.

My heart beat quickly, pleasurably!

Hours of the day each day trapped in my writing room, forced to work, or try to work, on the mystery novel formerly titled *Criss-Cross*, with damned little to show for it.

Nighttimes, writing as Jack of Spades, were much more productive.

But Andrew J. Rush was *me*. Damned if I would give up *me*.

Which is why I felt so—exhilarated! Outside in the night, invisible. In my dark disguise.

I'd known almost from the first what must be done. What reparations must be made to the wronged party.

I am not a common *thief.* I will admit, I was overcome by the rare books on C. W. Haider's shelves that looked as if they hadn't been opened in years; I'd given in to temptation, which was a mistake.

And so now, I was a repentant. Yet something of a coward too, for I'd hoped to return the purloined books to C. W. Haider weeks ago.

Since my first visit to 88 Tumbrel Place in September I'd been obsessively checking local media for news of C. W. Haider as well as tracking Stephen King online, to determine if (maybe) C. W. Haider had reacted in fury against Stephen King for the little prank I'd played on her in his name. Halfway I expected to see headlines—*Stephen King Threatened by New Jersey Stalker.* Better yet—*Stalker of Stephen King Arrested.*

Or—*Beloved Bestselling Novelist Stephen King Murdered by Madwoman Stalker.*

Or—*Madwoman Stalker Killed in Attempt on Life of Beloved Bestselling Novelist Stephen King.*

But none of this had happened. With each week that passed it was less likely to happen.

I could only assume that Haider had been discharged from the psychiatric hospital in New Brunswick weeks ago, and was living again at Tumbrel Place. Of course, I had no idea if she'd recovered from her derangement—perhaps she was still seriously ill. Perhaps she was in a clinically depressed state and had no interest in avenging herself on her old nemesis Stephen King, or anyone.

She might have undergone electric shock treatment. She might be massively sedated. By now, she might have totally forgotten Andrew J. Rush.

In the *Harbourton Weekly* there'd been no news of a robbery at 88 Tumbrel Place. Each issue I read eagerly and with dread, sure that I would see an accusatory headline—*Rare Books Stolen from Tumbrel Place Residence—Police Investigating Rare Book Theft from Haider Residence*—but again, there'd been nothing.

Had Haider not noticed the gaping absences on her bookshelves? Had I so cunningly covered my tracks, there was not much to notice? It seemed implausible that a collector who

owned such valuable books could be so negligent, but then
C. W. Haider was an enigma to me. I had no right to imagine
her as some sort of (reasonable, rational) extension of myself.

And so, it was my plan to return to the house by night, and
to replace the missing books unobtrusively, carried in my duffel
bag. *Frankenstein, The Lair of the White Worm, The Turn of the
Screw,* Le Fanu's *In a Glass Darkly* and one other, Wells's *The
Island of Dr. Moreau.*

And, not least, though I'd come to be particularly fond of it,
the slender *Imp of the Perverse.*

C. W. Haider's own novella *The Glowering,* which so curiously
anticipated King's *The Shining,* I'd decided to keep since there
were spare copies of the novella in Haider's bookshelf and she
would certainly never miss one.

Indeed, a long-unpublished writer like C. W. Haider would
be flattered to know that a long-established writer like Andrew
J. Rush cared to take the time to read her vanity-press effort.

Fortunately I must have anticipated returning to the house
back in September, and had unlocked two windows.

Not you, Andy. Don't deceive yourself.

You would ask—why didn't I simply just mail the purloined
books back to their owner? Of course, I had thought of this.
But to mail them to C. W. Haider via the U.S. Postal Service,
or UPS or FedEx, even to leave them carefully wrapped on the
front step, would be to call the excitable Haider's attention to
the fact that the books had been taken; and it was quite possible

that, in ill health, distracted by a hundred chimeras, Haider had not noticed their absence. The infuriated woman would then question her caretaker Esdra Staples, and the poor man would be incriminated for having allowed a thief into the house; possibly, Esdra could provide Haider with a detailed description of the gentlemanly middle-aged book thief which Haider might give to Harbourton police.

Not that anyone would pay the slightest attention to C. W. Haider's paranoia. Andrew J. Rush in particular had "immunity" from the woman's imaginary charges. Haider was a local crank known to law enforcement and the judiciary: Grossman had secured an injunction against her, to prevent her harassing *me*.

This was an act of mercy, kindness. I did not want to think that it was a reckless act which I might regret.

For some time now, Jack of Spades had been silent. When I anticipated his jeering wit, often there was silence.

Had he abandoned me? Was that a good thing?

My drinking was limited to a glass or two of white wine at dinner. No longer was there whiskey in the house. Irina seemed less wary of me, lately. We were lovers again—or nearly. For our thirtieth wedding anniversary we were planning a long-deferred trip to Spain. I was planning to buy her a beautiful black pearl necklace. Our sons, from whom I'd been somewhat estranged, for no reason I could comprehend, were friendlier now, at least in their e-mails and text messages.

Take care! A misstep now could be fatal.

Of course, I didn't park anywhere near the dignified old Edwardian house, which looked like a mausoleum by night. In fact, the entire neighborhood looked like a graveyard of large, ornate sepulchers.

There were a few scattered lights shimmering in the dark. But they were dim lights, that didn't "light up" any significant space. I carried a flashlight with a powerful but narrow beam, which I took care to use sparingly.

Swiftly and silently I made my way from the wrought iron gate and across the darkened lawn. And along the side of the house, ducking evergreen boughs. My breath steamed faintly in the sharp cold air. The narrow little beam of light guided me faultlessly, like a laser.

And here was the unlocked window! With some effort, I managed to open it, just enough to allow me to crawl through. Luckily there were several large clay pots at the side of the house which I could stand on, to get sufficient leverage.

And now—I was inside the house! The laser-light was ideal to guide me past furniture draped in ghostly shrouds. Though I was somewhat short of breath I made my way unerringly to the rear of the house, to Haider's writing room. The smells here were familiar, half-pleasurable. It seemed very recently that I'd been in this room, dazzled by what I'd found on the shelves.

I reasoned that C. W. Haider was sleeping in a remote room upstairs. I felt certain that the woman slept a heavy, drugged sleep. And she was alone in this house of course.

It had been my plan to return the books to their proper places on the shelves, and to depart. If nothing went wrong the intrusion wouldn't require more than ten minutes.

But now that I was here, in this forbidden place, I could not resist seeking out, with the laser-light, another title on the shelf which I coveted—the volume of *Dracula* which I knew to be a first edition signed by Bram Stoker.

How badly I wanted this book! And yet . . .

Take it. Quick!

Don't be a fool, you deserve this.

The volume of *Dracula* was in my hand, and in the duffel bag.

Next, I was captivated by an unprepossessing volume which another, less discerning eye would overlook—*The Dance of Death* by Ambrose Bierce. Excitedly, I opened the dingy volume to discover that it was a first edition—1877—inscribed and signed by Bierce himself.

My several Bierce books are second or third editions, not rare, and not signed.

"I must have this."

(Ambrose Bierce was one of the writers I'd read with particular excitement and admiration when I was just starting to write.)

And so, there came to be another volume in the duffel bag, with the others I'd intended to bring back to Haider.

Somehow it was happening, without my having quite decided it, that I wasn't returning the books to Haider's shelves after all. And I was feeling quite jubilant!

Of course. This is why you are here. Take what you wish, there is no one to stop you.

As I directed the beam of light about the high-ceilinged room—horizontally along the bookshelves, then vertically; across the desk that held the formidable old Remington typewriter; across the wide width of the fieldstone fireplace—I saw, or thought I saw, a movement in the corner of my eye near the floor; but when I turned, the shadowy figure vanished.

I reasoned that it was nothing—"notional." An effect of the flashlight beam causing shadows.

Next, I investigated Haider's desk. Here was a true old antique of a desk—once, a beautiful piece of furniture, a gentleman's desk; now rather battered and scarified. I saw that many of the keys in the typewriter were worn smooth, so that you could not discern the letters; I saw indentations in the keys worn by the typist's sharp fingernails, and shuddered at the prospect; I saw that there were deep rings and stains on the mahogany surface, as if the writer had carelessly set down cups and glasses. Before I could stop myself I glanced at the title of a manuscript placed on the desk—fortunately it was no title of mine, nor one I would be likely to appropriate: *Scourge of Hell.*

Though there was something teasingly familiar about the title, which slipped my mind for the moment.

I remembered that one of the desk drawers contained some intriguing personal material of Haider's. By flashlight I investigated notes, outlines, isolated manuscript pages, newspaper clippings, family photographs . . . Again, I was conscious of something, or someone, in the room, and when I turned quickly with the flashlight, a pair of gold-glaring eyes were illuminated.

A hoarse cry erupted—*Yyyoww*.

"Satan! Damn you."

Fortunately the cat's cry wasn't loud but rather insinuating, intimate. Where a dog would have barked ferociously to wake his mistress, and to frighten away an intruder, the sleek black cat was not greatly concerned, only rather intrigued by what I, his newfound friend, was doing.

"Would you like to come home with me? Eh, Satan? You are a beauty. Poe would have loved *you*."

(It is not like me to talk to animals. In fact, I think that people who talk to animals are silly. But here, somehow, in the excite-ment and tension of the moment, I found myself speaking, in a barely audible voice, to Haider's cat as if we were co-conspirators.)

When I leaned over to pet Satan's head, however, Satan shrank away like an ordinary cat, bristling his back, and emitted again, a little louder, the chilling caterwaul—*Yyyow*.

"Shhh! You know I won't hurt *you*."

I'd been removing manila folders from the drawer to sift through. I was noticing that a number of Haider's photographs, which dated back to the 1920s, were of quite striking individuals; there was a common Haider prototype, with a hawkish profile, a pronounced forehead, sharp accusatory eyes and sardonic mouth. In several photographs were individuals of indeterminate sex with white hair like Haider's, that seemed to stand out from their heads as if electrified.

I selected a number of family photographs out of the drawer to drop into my duffel bag. Though I could not have said why, I thought that these personal artifacts could be precious to me; there were sections in *Criss-Cross* that needed amplifying with more engaging and original characters, which these photos might suggest. Also, I took a sheaf of plot outlines. Surely, Haider would never miss these.

Now, you should leave. Do not stay a moment longer.

Indeed, I was ready to retreat. The duffel bag was filled almost to capacity. But now I'd noticed on the ash-strewn floor near the fireplace, beside the ax and the brass andirons, a stack of cardboard files with sliding drawers. These I recognized as files Haider had brought to the courthouse containing what she'd believed to be damning evidence against Andrew J. Rush. I felt a leap of fear, and also of excitement.

No. No time. Leave these.

But I could not leave!—not without investigating these files. And they were too bulky to take with me, along with the spoils I already had. The flashlight I could shove into a pocket, but the other items were too large.

Awkwardly I squatted beside the files. With a tug I managed to slide open one of the drawers.

In the too-bright light from the flashlight Haider's meticu-lously hand-lettered white note cards were almost unreadable. Were these passages from my books, set beside passages from hers? Was this the "proof" Judge Carson had tossed out of court?

Maybe I could take some of the cards, a handful at least. Or maybe—I could plan to return to the house another time.

No. Hurry. You must leave—now . . .

But somehow, though I understood that I was in danger, and should flee while I could, I did not move. Squatting, hunched over, in a most vulnerable posture I was frowning over this fascinating material, when something nudged against my ankles—the bone-hard head of Satan. Naïvely I reached out to pet the beautiful creature, thinking that he was indeed a co-conspirator, and wished me well; but felt a sudden rake of claws against the back of my hand, penetrating my glove—"God *damn*"—and suddenly, in an instant, chaos seemed to erupt like an exploding ꜱꜱꜱꜱ ꜱꜱꜱ ꜱꜱ ꜱꜱꜱ ꜱꜱꜱꜱ.

"Thief! Scoundrel!"—the hoarse voice was unmistakable, close behind me.

Out of the air, the ax. Somehow there was an ax and it rose and fell in a wild swath aimed at my head even as I tried to rise from my squatting position and lost my balance desperate to escape as my legs faltered beneath me and there came a hoarse pleading voice—"No! No please! No"—(was this my own choked voice, unrecognizable?)—as the ax-blade crashed and sank into the splintering desk beside my head, missing my head by inches; by which time I'd fallen heavily onto the floor, a hard unyielding floor beneath the frayed Oriental carpet. I was scrambling to right myself, grabbing for the ax (that was wielded, I could see now, by the wild-white-haired woman, her face distorted by a look of maniacal hatred), desperate to seize the ax, in the blindness of desperation my hands flailing, and the voice (my own? my assailant's?) high-pitched and hardly human-sounding—"No! *Nooo*"—a fleeting glimpse of the assailant's stubby fingers and dead-white ropey-muscled arms inside the flimsy sleeves of nightwear, and a grunting cry as of triumph and fury commingled as the ax was wrested to another's stronger hands; and again the terrible lifting of the ax-head, the dull sheen of the crude ax-blade, and the downward swing of Death once begun unstoppable, irretrievable plunging into a human skull as easily rent as a melon with no more protection than a thick rind, to expose the pulpy gray-matter of the brain amid a torrential gushing of arterial blood.

And still the voice rising disbelieving *No no no no no.*

20   10-Year-Old Harbourton Boy
Drowns in Quarry,
Catamount Park. July 1973.

No one blamed me.
No one blamed me to my face.

21   Lynx. November 2014.

"Andrew! There's more of the terrible news here."

Irina lay the newspaper in front of me, with its lurid banner headline—the first such headline I'd ever seen in the staid *Harbourton Weekly*.

HAIDER HEIRESS MURDERED
IN TUMBREL PLACE HOME
Break-in, Robbery Motive
Suspects Questioned

We were at our breakfast table in a glassed-in porch adjacent to our kitchen. Through a haze of headache pain my eyes could barely make out the printed words and the somber photograph of *Corin Wren Haider* that had been taken years ago. A sixty-eight-year-old woman who'd lived alone in one of the grand old houses in Tumbrel Square, Harbourton, since her father's death in 2003, murdered by an ax-wielding assailant who was believed to have broken into her house sometime after midnight with the intention of robbery.

An ax attack! Irina shuddered, standing behind me.

We had been seeing TV news of the local, brutal murder for several days by the time of the *Harbourton Weekly* publication. I had been hearing radio updates, "breaking news."

"The poor woman! You'd said she was mentally unstable. She shouldn't have been living alone. And how awful, that someone who'd worked for her family, for so long, might be the murderer."

It was noted that Harbourton detectives were questioning employees of the Haider family. Relatives of the deceased woman were quoted saying that Ms. Haider frequently kept "large sums of money" scattered through her house, out of a distrust of banks. Though few details had been released to the media I knew from a contact at Harbourton police headquarters that the caretaker, who'd worked for the Haiders since 1985, was the prime suspect.

This was stunning news. This was the truly upsetting news in the *Harbourton Weekly.*

Look, it isn't your fault. Andrew J. Rush is not to blame.

You had no choice, it was your life or hers.

Irina was murmuring what a coincidence it was, that the murdered woman was the very person who'd tried to sue me! And what an unhappy person she must have been, living alone in that mansion.

"Evidently 'C. W. Haider' had written for the *Harbourton Weekly* and other local publications, years ago. She'd reported on the 'arts' and wrote book reviews . . . Oh! Look at her picture, here—taken in 1963. She was quite striking even before her hair turned white."

Irina had turned to an inside page. Columns of newspaper blurred in my vision. I shut my eyes, for I did not want to see.

It is not your fault—remember that.

Don't weaken! Don't be a coward.

You took the ax from her in self-defense. Beyond that—you have nothing to repent.

Irina continued to speak of the "terrible, terrifying" murder. The last such violent incident in Harbourton had happened in 1971—a drunken fight that had resulted in a wife being shoved through a plate glass sliding door. But nowhere near Tumbrel Place.

"Evidently, Ms. Haider 'feuded' with her neighbors. And she'd initiated 'many lawsuits' over the years."

Through the throbbing pain in my head I found it difficult to listen to my wife.

You did the right thing. No jury would convict.

No jury would blame Andrew J. Rush.

Since that night, Jack of Spades intruded into my thoughts persistently. For I had no other counsel.

No blame. No blame. No blame.

Shame!

Unpredictably Jack of Spades spoke. At times his voice was thrilling, supportive. At other times, mocking.

Shame shame shame shame.

Yet Andy is not to blame.

JOYCE CAROL OATES

"Andrew, darling?"—Irina's voice was tense—"what did you say?"

"What did I say? I'm sure I didn't say anything."

There was a pause. Irina meant to speak but thought better of it. Quickly we finished with the newspaper. No more ax-murder for a while!

"Well. Shall I get us some coffee?"

"Yes, darling. Please."

Irina went away. Such relief!

Thinking of how, that night, just a few nights ago, I'd managed to escape from the blood-drenched scene.

Astonishing to me now, in the seclusion and quiet of our beautiful glassed-in porch at Mill Brook House, that I had been capable of such action, in such desperate circumstances, so recently. That I, who was feeling now so lethargic, had been able to wrench the ax from Haider's hands, and break her grip, and seize the ax handle in my own hands, and wield it—*Not you who seized the ax, not you but another whose strength coursed into your body and redeemed it.*

Obsessively I'd tried to comprehend: Haider had been wakened from her sleep in an upstairs room, and had come downstairs silently to confront the intruder. No normal woman—no normal citizen of Harbourton—would have behaved so recklessly, and so vengefully. She had not been frightened for a moment. She had not called 911. *She had wanted to attack with the ax.*

Many times since the incident I'd wondered if in the dim light she'd recognized Andrew J. Rush from his author photo. If she'd been surprised, or not surprised.

174

I had been very quiet entering the house. I had been very quiet throughout. It must have been the malicious Satan who'd alerted his mistress.

While I was examining the bookshelves, sleek black Satan had slipped away upstairs to waken Haider, and summon her downstairs to her death.

Why had she given no warning? Why had she not screamed at the intruder, to frighten him away? To save her own life?

She had been the one to want to crush a skull with the ax, in a vengeful rage. She'd screamed at me only when it was too late, when she was upon me—"Thief! Scoundrel!"

The madwoman is to blame, and not you.

Spotless as a lamb though blood-splattered.

After I wrenched the ax from the woman's hands it was not clear what happened next. Only vaguely was I aware of smiting her—raising the ax, bringing it down against the wild white hair—not to kill, but to save my own life.

A strangled cry from my own throat—*No no no no no.*

At once, there was wetness everywhere. A fierce hot blood-wetness, that spattered onto my face, clothes, gloved hands.

Even as I dropped the ax, the body fell. The wild-white-haired head seemed to sink onto the shoulders, skull split and gushing.

Frantic I may have tried to set her—the body—upright again. Tried to revive her—that is, it. But now a lifeless body heavy as a sack of concrete.

"No! I didn't mean it—please, no . . ."

(Did I speak aloud? Fortunately, Irina was in the kitchen orchestrating our elaborate coffee machine.)

But the woman—the body she'd become—had fallen, twisted upon itself on the floor, in nightclothes darkened with spreading blood. She who'd been so vituperative, so condemning, was now silent—silenced.

The crazed black cat was hissing at me from a few yards away, eyes glaring. If I'd had the ax in my hands I would have taken a swipe at it for I had a sudden mad wish to cut the jeering creature in two.

"You—*demon!*"

"And then, somehow I'd managed to escape—slipping in blood, gasping for breath, sobbing, shuddering—leaving the murder weapon behind, but having enough presence of mind to take my duffel bag, that was heavy with plunder, and the flashlight with its narrow, powerful beam—escaping not through the opened window in the drawing room but through a side door, that opened out of the kitchen into a pit of darkness beneath overgrown evergreens, and led to a path beside the house, that led in turn to the driveway.

My car was parked a half-block away on Tumbrel Square. At a corner of property owned by the Episcopal rectory.

Like an automaton I managed to drive my car through narrow deserted village streets, onto a deserted state highway and so into the countryside dark as a great ocean. By instinct making my way to Mill Brook Road and so to Mill Brook House where, in our darkened upstairs bedroom, at this hour of 1:40 A.M. Irina slept with no knowledge of any of this horror; and if she'd wakened, and saw that I wasn't beside her in bed, she would have supposed that I'd slipped away to work in another part of the house, having been unable to sleep.

Poor Andrew! He is so dedicated to his writing, that never seems to be going well though others, who scarcely know him, believe that he writes easily and without a backward glance.

Downstairs, in a guest room, I washed my face that had begun to stiffen with drying blood. I removed my blood-soaked shoes, stripped off my clothes, and rolled them into a bundle, and put the bundle in a large black plastic garbage bag, which I would dispose of the next day in a landfill twelve miles away.

Seeing then, to my horror, that the duffel bag too was soaked in blood, and adding this to the garbage bag.

Haider's photographs, notes, plot outlines—these I shoved into the garbage bag. But I could not force myself to discard the priceless books, for which I'd sacrificed so much.

After my exertions, I took a shower. I washed my hair, that had grown thin in recent years, in which there were snarls of dried blood. I scrubbed the back of my left hand, where Satan had raked me with his claws through my glove. In a closet, I found fresh clothes. I did not expect to sleep for all my senses were alert and aroused but lay atop the bed in the guest room, which smelled pleasantly of potpourri and expensive soap; so exhausted, I did manage to fall asleep at about four o'clock in the morning, and wakened abruptly at six o'clock, with a thudding heart.

For a moment, I had no idea where I was. I remembered nothing—my mind was blank.

Then, the horror washed over me, with a smell of marshy soil amid the oversweet potpourri and colored soap.

Quickly then I rose, and dressed, and went outside in the air that smelled of frost, and drove the Jaguar to the county landfill north of Hadrian, where as the sky lightened by quick degrees I hiked into the interior of mounds of trash, carrying the garbage bag. I was breathing quickly, panting. I was feeling strangely jubilant. Once I found a likely place to hide the bag, I untied it, and shoved into it miscellaneous articles of trash including broken children's toys—"That will confuse them!" Tightly I retied the bag, and hid it deep where it would never be found.

When I returned to Mill Brook House, I discovered to my horror that I'd left lights on in the guest room and adjoining bathroom. A smudge of something red on the bathroom tile floor, wiped up with a damp tissue.

It wasn't clear if Irina was up yet. Probably yes, since it was after 7:00 A.M. But I didn't hear a sound.

About the precious books: after all that I'd done to acquire them I decided not to hide them timidly away but to boldly display them upstairs, interspersed with my own, more modest collection. Henry James's *The Turn of the Screw* (signed first edition, 1898), for instance, would be shelved matter-of-factly beside *Ghost Stories of Henry James* (1961). Bram Stoker's *Dracula* (signed first edition, 1897) would be shelved beside the oversized glossy *Dracula in Hollywood* (1993). None of the news articles about the break-in and the ax-murder had mentioned stolen rare books which led me to assume that no one of Haider's relatives knew enough about the collection to notice that anything was missing, or to care.

Haider's relatives had been focused upon more vulgar sorts of theft—money. I had not cared in the slightest for all the money C. W. Haider might have secreted in her house and I felt contempt for the small-minded, who could imagine one might kill for *mere money*.

It was a pleasurable morning I spent alone in the house shelving my new books, while Irina was at the Friends School. On the time-worn covers of *In a Glass Darkly* and *The Island of Dr. Moreau* I discovered faint traces of a dark liquid which I simply rubbed away with a damp cloth—for books so old and so rare are not expected to be in pristine condition.

"No one will know. These are books I might easily have purchased."

To the victor, the spoils.

"Look, Andrew! Is that a cat, or a lynx?"

Irina had just returned with a tray bearing our coffee in mugs. Excitedly she pointed out the window at a sleek black-furred creature about one hundred feet from the house, making its leisurely way across our field of vision. It was a large black cat—unless it was a wild cat, a lynx—an "endangered" species in this part of New Jersey.

"How beautiful!" Irina cried. "But I hope it won't attack the birds at our feeders."

As I stared, the creature disappeared into shrubbery at the side of the house, without a sidelong glance.

22 The Guilty Party

Strange how, when I could not work as Andrew J. Rush, and could not sleep, I could write for hours in a kind of delirium as Jack of Spades.

Pages whipped past. My breath was quickened.

You have tapped the jugular!

No turning back.

Strange too, how I thought most guiltily of Esdra Staples and not of C. W. Haider whose skull I cracked with the crude dull edge of the ax.

Or, rather, Haider's skull had been cracked with the plunging ax whose handle my hands had gripped. I could recall no volition, no decision to strike the woman even in self-defense.

This happened, and I was the agent. But I did not cause it to happen.

As long ago I had crept out onto the high diving board at the Catamount quarry to goad—to touch—lightly!—my brother Evan with just two fingers in the small of his back.

His screams on the (brief) way down. His screams that have split my skull but only emptiness has streamed out.

By late November the caretaker Esdra Staples had been arrested in the Tumbrel Place ax murder. Much of (white) Harbourton had come to assume that the (black) man was the murderer.

What a pity!—a (hyper-vigilant, racist?) Tumbrel Place neighbor reported to police that she had seen a "shadowy, dark-skinned figure" making his way up the front walk of the Haider house on the night of the ax-murder, to knock at the door . . . My dark-clothed disguise had persuaded the old fool to imagine that I was myself *dark-skinned*; and *dark-skinned* could only mean, in the ambiance of mostly white Harbourton, the suspect Esdra Staples.

"Esdra! I am *so sorry*."

Soon after the news broke, Grossman called me.

I'd known that Grossman would call eventually. My jaws ground my back teeth in exasperation and fury, there was no way to prevent the unwanted intrusion from the brash Manhattan lawyer.

"Andrew, what a surprise! I saw the item by chance, online. 'Haider'—the name wouldn't have meant anything to me otherwise."

Vaguely I murmured a reply. Yes. That is—no.

My mouth had gone dry. It was very difficult to speak.

I'd broken into the woman's place to return her books, not to steal her books. I'd broken her skull not to kill her but to prevent her killing me.

Please believe me!

(I had not fantasized confessing to Grossman—had I?)

(Jack of Spades would not allow such cowardice!)

Grossman was marveling at the bizarre murder, of so bizarre an individual.

"One of the family employees killed her, police think? Probably couldn't take it any longer, the old witch giving him orders."

Grossman seemed to be inviting me to laugh with him but I remained silent. I had answered the call reluctantly seeing the lawyer's name on the ID screen. In my writing room I was sitting on a chair leaning far forward, elbows on my knees. My face was contorted, my jaws moving. I had to hope that I wasn't saying anything to Grossman that I didn't want the lawyer to hear.

Grossman said, marveling, "Only in one of the longer news articles was it mentioned that Haider had sued so many writers. Of course, it was Stephen King who was named—poor Steve! Next thing, a rumor will circulate that Stephen King came secretly to Harbourton, broke into her house and killed his stalker."

Grossman laughed, cruelly. But why was this funny?

"Elliot, it's a terrible situation. I'm very sorry that that poor woman had to die in such a way. Of course, I suppose I'm relieved—as I'm relieved that my name hasn't turned up yet in the news articles. There's an advantage to being less famous than Stephen King . . . But here's my concern: the caretaker is an elderly black man who'd worked for the family for thirty years. He's certainly innocent. If an employee of Haider's wanted to rob her he could have done it at any time, and not when she was in the house. And not in the middle of the night, or whenever this happened. And not with an ax. For why murder Haider at all, if all he wanted was her money?"

Grossman must have been impressed by this outburst, or astonished. For the first time in my experience with the lawyer he had no ready reply. Quickly I continued:

"And so I was thinking, Elliot—the man needs a lawyer to defend him. He's black, he'll be railroaded into a conviction. I don't know Esdra Staples—of course—I never knew *her*—but whoever killed Haider, he'd have had to be from the outside, not an employee; the killer came through a window he'd forced open, which the caretaker wouldn't have had to do." I paused, breathing hard. How clever I was! For the window had not been "forced open" as I well knew—it had simply been opened. And when I'd fled in a panic, I hadn't returned to shut the window which had been pushed open sufficiently to have allowed an adult male to crawl through.

All this, I told Grossman, I'd been reading in the *Harbourton Weekly*. No one was talking about anything else here in Harbourton—the last violent death had been in 1971, and that had been manslaughter.

"Could you help me with this, Elliot? Find a good lawyer for the caretaker, and I'll pay his fee?"

How lavish I was feeling! At least, it was a good, buoyant feeling for once.

Grossman responded dubiously. A lawyer for a stranger? Why'd I want to be involved?

"Because it's the right thing to do. I know that the man will be railroaded into a conviction here in Hecate County and I want to prevent that if I can."

"But you say you don't know him—?"

"How would I know Haider's caretaker? You know—I've never met *her*."

This was true. I had spoken, pleaded, with C. W. Haider on the phone, and I had wrested an ax from her fingers and split her skull with it, but I had not met her.

I told Grossman that the murder had surely been by chance—someone had broken into the house, looking for money, and Haider had confronted him, unwisely. "The police have no leads so they've arrested poor Esdra Staples. Supposedly, he was the last person to have seen Haider alive except for the killer."

Grossman was silent. I broke into a sweat worrying that in my zeal to defend Esdra Staples, I had exposed a fatal vulnerability in myself. Grossman would become suspicious, and his suspicions would turn upon *me*.

Except, Grossman said, thoughtfully: "Or—it's one of the heirs. A relative in the old woman's will, impatient for her to die."

We talked for a while longer. Grossman agreed to contact a New Jersey lawyer skilled in criminal defense to take on the case, if the caretaker agreed.

After we hung up, I felt as if a great weight had been lifted from me.

Staggering to my feet, weak-kneed, but suffused with hope.

23   Predator

"Satan! Go back to hell where you belong."

Running behind the house with my newly purchased
.22-caliber rifle aimed at the sleek black creature thirty feet
away daring to pause at a corner of the barn, to glare back at
me with mocking eyes, and I stumbled in the ice-stiffened grass,
turned an ankle and fell hard and the shot rang out loud enough
to deafen me for a stunned moment thinking—*Am I shot? Am
I alive—or still dead?*

24   Unrepentant Son

"Andrew, I'm afraid there's bad news. Your father is not doing well."

With care Irina chose her words. For Irina well knew how sensitive I'd become these past several months.

"Your mother called just now. She's saying she hopes that we will come to see your father in the hospice before—it's too late."

Hospice? There is no exit from *hospice* except one.

Irina saw the shock in my face. And also the distrust, suspicion.

"But why didn't you tell me earlier, Irina?—you and Mom?"

Strangely comforting to utter the word *Mom*. For a man who'd just turned fifty-four.

"But I did tell you, Andrew. I tried to tell you . . ."

"When?"

"When your father had those tests back in April—you know, at Robert Wood Johnson Medical Center. And then the surgery, and the chemotherapy . . ."

"No. No one told me."

"But, Andrew—I'm sure that I told you, your father was moved to the Falls Ridge hospice last week . . ."

Pleadingly Irina regarded me as if she might inveigle the reasonable husband Andrew to conspire with her against the unreasonable husband Andrew—*me*!

"I said—*no one told me*. At least, no one kept me informed on Dad's progress. Or lack of progress. Or how serious it all was—is. You certainly didn't, darling."

Yet, was this true? Vaguely I seemed to know that my father *was not doing well* for some time.

Driving on our country roads you see the carcasses of animals—raccoons, deer—lying at the roadside, killed by vehicles. But you don't turn your eyes that way, by instinct.

Not doing well can mean so many things. Best not to inquire.

But I did recall, so vividly that my heart began to pound with resentment, how, the last time we went to visit my parents—(Christmas? birthday?)—who lived only seven miles away, there was some problem with my father who hadn't been home.

Or, if Dad had been home Dad hadn't wished to see us.

That is, hadn't wished to see *me*.

My face began to flush at the memory, pounding with heat. Why was this disturbing memory forced upon me, like something ugly shoved into my mouth?

She wants to unsettle you. The woman.

Wants to emasculate you. Like the other—the enemy.

190

It was always unsettling when Irina entered my writing room even when she'd knocked quietly at the door. When she had something of such urgency to tell me she didn't feel she could send an e-mail or use the intercom phone.

But I'd come to hate a ringing phone. It was rare that I would consent to answer a ringing phone even if my editor was calling.

Hadn't I tried to explain to Irina that I preferred her to contact me via e-mail rather than barge into my solitude and disrupt my work?—but this was a special situation, I suppose. *My father is dying and has refused to see me for years and I am expected to care?*

Fact is, I did care. I was feeling weak and ill, with caring.

"Irina, the last time I tried to see Dad, remember he'd 'gone out for a walk' and didn't return."

"Yes, but—your mother thinks he would like to see you now . . ."

"He doesn't want to see me. He's pretending to be demented."

"Andrew, you gave up too soon when he started behaving the way he did. It is 'dementia'—but he has interludes of lucidity, your mother says. I've talked to him myself, on the phone . . ."

"*You've* talked to him? Since when?"

"I'm sure you've known, Andrew. I keep in touch with your parents—I've told you. Your mother and I are very close."

"Since when?"

"Well, since—the past few years . . ."

"Is it my mother who says that I 'gave up too soon' with Dad? Am I supposed to crawl like a penitent and kiss his foot? Beg to be forgiven for something that didn't happen, forty-one years five months ago?"

My voice was aggrieved, anguished. The voice of the twelve-year-old of whom it was whispered behind his back *That's him. That's the one.*

"Your mother thinks that now, now that he's in the hospice, he will be more realistic about seeing you. We could go together tonight."

"Tonight! Not possible."

"Well—tomorrow . . ."

"Look, Irina—for thirty years it was all right between us. I mean—Dad had behaved as if it was all right. He accepted it had been an accident with my brother—he knew how devastated I was—so why'd he change his mind? That's what infuriates me."

"He's an elderly man, Andrew. It was the beginning of the change in him, when he began to"—Irina paused, searching for the most diplomatic way of expressing my father's sudden repugnance for the sight of my face and the sound of my voice—"feel less comfortable around you. Your mother thinks he'd had a stroke that went undiagnosed, about six years ago . . ."

Irina spoke carefully. Defending my father.

Yet, because she loved me, at the same time defending *me.*

Of course Irina knew about Evan. All there was to know about Evan.

One day, I'd had to tell her. Confess, confide in her.

When we'd decided to get married. When it was clear that, if I didn't tell her, someone else would.

Midway in my telling, my words had seemed to give out.

There was no way to speak of it. There had never been any way to speak of it.

He lost his balance on the high diving board, and fell.

It was an accident, no one was to blame.

We'd been swimming in the quarry at Catamount Park and then I climbed up over the rocks to a place where the water was deeper and there was a makeshift diving board about fifteen feet above the water.

Older guys hung out there. Never any girls, or kids Evan's age. Why'd he follow me! I told him to go back.

Most of the guys didn't dive but just jumped off the board. That was all I did—held my nose and jumped. And Evan was going to jump but at the end of the board he froze. Guys were yelling at him to jump and I was embarrassed of my kid brother and started out onto the board but I wasn't going to push him of course. I'd been just kidding of course. Had not pushed him—of course.

If I'd touched him it was just with two fingers in the small of his back to give him a little nudge he was taking too long.

Must've panicked and lost his balance and fell sideways and hit his head on the edge of the diving board, hit the water at an angle that exacerbated the fracture—skinny kid who could swim like a fish but limp now, lifeless—sinking in the deep quarry water like a rock—never breathed again.

Witnesses said different things but the ruling was, accident.
Rush brothers. Twelve, ten.
Andrew, Evan. Where both were beloved, now there was but one.

In the end, Irina went alone to the hospice.
Could not risk being rejected by my father another time.
Is it lonely, yes it is lonely. Through the years it has been lonely.
I think of how Evan would have loved many things in the world he had not yet seen. And it was not my fault but yet—it was my fault.
The fact is, it was ruled an accident.
No one blamed me.
No one blamed me to my face.

25 Good News!

But there was good news for Jack of Spades.

The new novel *Scourge* received starred reviews in several publications and online—now reviewers were comparing Jack of Spades to Stephen King!

A more visceral, take-no-prisoners Stephen King.

Move over, Stephen King! Jack of Spades is on the scene.

Also, there was enthusiasm among booksellers—orders were reportedly higher than for any previous title by Jack of Spades.

(Embarrassingly near the orders for Andrew Rush's most recent book, in fact.)

Was this funny? Was this *ironic*?

Should I have felt pride, or chagrin?

Since the ax attack—(I'd come to think of the violent episode in Haider's house as an attack upon my person, essentially—which I'd had to defend myself against)—my ability to concentrate had perceptibly deteriorated. My ability to see the "humor" in most things, indeed the "happiness" in things.

Admit it, Andy Rush: you're jealous of Jack of Spades.
And thrilled, and a little scared.
Yes?

"This 'Jack of Spades'!—he's *disgusting*."

By chance I happened to overhear my daughter Julia complaining to Irina about—evidently—another novel she'd just read by the "mystery author," obviously without my encouragement. It was a source of dismay to me, and some resentment, that my fastidious feminist-daughter persisted in reading what she called "macho-sadist trash," presumably in order to denounce it, while she never took time to read my far more serious and uplifting mystery novels in which evil people were duly punished and "good" people rewarded.

How I wished I'd quickly stored away those damned paperbacks of Jack of Spades, that Julia had seen in my writing room months ago! It had been sheer carelessness on my part to leave them in plain sight.

Come off it, Andy. You'd wanted your beloved daughter to see my books. You'd have liked Irina to notice too, but your wife has other things on her mind these days—and nights.

The voice was jeering, confiding. Though I knew that it was not truly a "voice" yet I stood very still, head lowered, listening.

You know that, Andy—don't you?

No. Did not know.

Sure you do. Irina and her Asian lover.

In the other room Julia was describing to Irina the "preposter-ous plot" of *Prepostmortem,* and Irina seemed to be listening. Or maybe Irina, mind elsewhere, wasn't listening to our daughter's vehement objections but only politely murmuring in response.

Prepostmortem was the second title by Jack of Spades, or maybe the third. Offhand, I couldn't have given the publication date. The plot, like the title, had come to me out of nowhere.

"I tried to tell Daddy but he refused to listen. Whoever this 'Jack of Spades' is, he must know Daddy and his family. The other novel I read was vicious enough but this is worse! The story is about a teenaged boy who 'accidentally' kills his younger brother by pushing him off a high diving board in a quarry—then, he's 'devastated by grief'—but relieved too, because he'd been jealous of his brother. The family is divided between those who believe the boy when he says it was an accident and those who don't believe him but think he pushed his brother into the water deliberately. In the present time, he's middle-aged and married to a woman he insists he loves very much but he's very jealous of her and tries to find a way to kill her 'accidentally' . . . That part seems just fiction but the backstory, about the boy drowning in a quarry, in a park in New Jersey, has got to be based on what happened to Daddy when he was a boy and his brother accidentally drowned at Catamount Park. I don't know the details, Mom, but it has got to be more than just a coincidence, don't you think?"

"Well, Julia. I haven't read the novel, and from what you've been saying I don't think that I want to. That accident in the quarry at Catamount—when your father was twelve—was reported in the local papers and anyone in this part of New Jersey would have known about it. What's your point, 'more than coincidence'?"

"I think there's some person Daddy knows, one of his writer-friends, who is using Daddy's life to write about, but distorting it and making it ugly, with lots more detail and background than you could get from just the media. And Daddy doesn't seem to know about it, or to care. I tried to get him to read the other novel by Jack of Spades, but he refused. He just says it's a coincidence, and not important. But I think . . ."

"Why not just throw out the trashy books, Julia? Even if they are based on some parts of your father's life, how does that affect you, or any of us? Maybe your father does know the writer, and maybe your father is upset and angry, but you know that your father wouldn't try to censor anyone."

"Of course Daddy wouldn't try to 'censor' anyone. But he should be careful what he tells this person, who's like a vampire feeding on Daddy's life."

"Oh Julia, do you believe in 'vampires'?"—Irina laughed, reprovingly.

"I never used to. But now, lately, I'm not too sure."

"But what could Andrew do, to stop this person? Assuming there is a 'vampire' in his life?"

"What could Daddy *do*? That's up to Daddy."

26   "2 Dark 4 Me"

At the Hadrian, New Jersey, post office I mailed a neatly taped, small box of five paperback books addressed to Stephen King at his home in Maine.

The inscriptions were block-printed in a hand that seemed (to me) quite different from my own.

With Admiration—to Stephen King—

Your Rival-One-Day—

"Jack of Spades"

The return address was the P.O. box in Hadrian which I rented. Not that I expected the very busy bestselling author to respond to some unsolicited paperback books by a little-known writer as King had not responded to a similar cache by Andrew J. Rush.

Imagine my surprise and chagrin when, a few weeks later, a hastily scrawled postcard arrived at the P.O. addressed to "Jack of Spades."

Whoever you are—"Jack of Spades"—U R 2 DARK 4 Me & We ARE NOT rivals

S.K.

27   Jealous Husband

Admit it, Andy. You are damned jealous.
Jealous of Jack of Spades, and of the woman.
And the Asian, what's-his-name—HUANG LEE.

Not to my wife's face was I jealous. Not a hint!

A bruised heart is not visible, like a bruised face.

"I love you, Irina. I don't know what I would do without you . . ."

"But Andrew, don't be silly! Why would you be 'without me'?"

And Irina kissed me, and we staggered in a sudden embrace.

On my breath, Irina may have smelled whiskey. In the soft waves of her hair, I may have smelled perfume.

At this time, Irina was often away in the evenings. I did not always know where she was though (I suppose) she took care to tell me. Leaving food prepared for me in the refrigerator which all I had to do (as she said) was heat in the microwave.

Might be, the woman is poisoning you.

Arsenic can poison by slow degrees. Its symptoms can be many things.

Out of spite as well as caution I scraped the woman's food into the garbage disposal. A quick call, and I could have a decent dinner delivered to the house, or better yet the hell with food. Scotch whiskey has a way of placating a man's appetite.

But when I confronted Irina about the frequency of evening meetings at the Friends School she was likely to tell me in her gently reproving way that she hadn't been at the school but, as she'd explained, visiting with my mother who felt "alone and abandoned" since my father's death.

Or, if I seemed to recall that Irina was visiting my mother, and I called her cell phone, there was no answer because Irina wasn't at my mother's but at a meeting at the school at which cell phones had to be shut off.

Or, she was spending the night with her own family, in Montclair.

Or, having dinner in Newark with Chris, or with Dale.

(Why Dad wasn't included in these dinners with our sons was not clear. But Dad had too much pride to inquire, thank you.)

"Andrew, I told you where I was going. Shall I write these things down, and leave numbers?"

Yes. No.

Why should you care what the woman does?

Is it your fatal weakness, that you do?

28   "Damn Your Soul to Hell"

Returning home early one evening on Mill Brook Road in a lightly falling rain and seeing about thirty feet in front of my car a dark-furred animal of the size of a fox or a lynx crossing the road at a slow trot. Seeing me, its tawny eyes blazed in my headlights with a look of animal cunning or defiance.

"God damn your soul to hell!"—the voice was furious and aggrieved and like no voice of my own with which I was familiar.

My first instinct was to brake my car and swerve to avoid hitting the animal—(and risk killing myself in a crash)—but my second instinct, far shrewder, was to continue without turning my steering wheel even a fraction of an inch and even (perhaps) to press down harder on the gas pedal.

The front wheels struck—something . . . I felt the brief impact, that reverberated through my spine like an electrical current.

Yet somehow, though (I'm sure) I had not increased my speed by more than ten miles an hour, the Jaguar went into a spin on the wet pavement, and within the confusion of a few seconds the Jaguar was on its side in a ditch.

Fortunately, my vehicle hadn't crashed into a fence post. The impact might have thrown the reckless driver against the windshield and knocked him unconscious.

When I recovered my wits I managed to force the car door open. On shaky legs I staggered squinting along the edge of the road.

Indeed there was something crushed and flattened at the roadside, a small dark-furred corpse.

But it was not quivering with the last vestiges of life, or bleeding. Its eyes were open yet not tawny with the defiance of life.

Whatever the creature was, it had been there for days, badly flattened and decomposing, unrecognizable.

Fool! You are looking in the wrong place.

29 "Accident"

And now it's time—for Andy Rush to commit another perfect crime.

For months the idea had been gathering at the back of my mind like a small dense tumor. Each time I dared check the tumor it had grown a little larger, and denser.

It would be an accident—of course. Driving along a country road, and there's a bicyclist—and the vehicle "loses control"—swerves into the cyclist.

With no witness who is to say if the bicyclist had behaved recklessly? Bicycling in the road, making a sharp turn—that's it for *him*.

No longer did I inquire after "Huang Lee" when I spoke with my dear wife about the Friends School. For I knew that this person was my wife's lover and that I must not appear to be suspicious of him, or even aware of him.

But in the early hours of the morning as I hunched over Jack of Spades's writing table the pen in my hand block-printed

HUANG LEE

R.I.P.

in the form of a jocular gravestone epitaph.

It was known that the popular math teacher bicycled to school nearly every day and even, sometimes, in a lightly falling rain, at which time he wore a shiny yellow poncho. Only in winter, and when roads were near-impassable, did the lanky jet-black-haired Asian drive a car—of course, a gas-saving Honda Civic.

Carefully I calculated when Huang Lee was likely to be bi-cycling to/from the Friends School, and which route he would be taking on the commute of 3.8 miles.

Several times I drove along the likely roads, approaching the Lee house at 299 East Elm Ridge Road, in which the adul-terer (allegedly) lived with a wife and two young children, in a "middle-class" suburban neighborhood in Harbourton; several times, all I could do was drive past the house, into Harbourton, turn around and retrace my route, determined to remain calm.

Be patient. Take care. Time is on your side, Andy Rush!

On these drives, Jack of Spades was my companion.

How lonely, but for Jack of Spades!

And, secure between my knees, not visible to anyone who might glance in my direction, a small silver flask containing a very smooth-tasting liquid much recommended by Jack of Spades for the calming of frayed nerves.

It was a cool day, overcast. Few bicyclists on such a day in early spring and so, I reasoned, I would have little difficulty in sighting Huang Lee if/when I saw him.

Not a happy time for Andy Rush. Grinding my back teeth.

Even my dear adulterous wife was embarrassed by the degree to which our sons Chris and Dale had become "estranged" from their father. I'm not sure how it happened. Or even when.

Damned spoiled kids disrespecting their father who'd done so much for them . . .

I'd known that something was fishy, both of them showing up for Sunday supper—as if by accident. And Irina smiling too much.

Jack of Spades slipped me off early. Sharp-eyed Jack of Spades noting how the boys were exchanging glances with each other and with their mother.

Jesus! This conversation is what you'd call A W K W A R D.

Be alert, friend. Watch your back.

Maybe the disrespect begins with the son growing taller than the father. Is there an actual day, an actual *hour,* when the heights are reversed?

In photos, you can see the kids growing. In life, you can't.

By this time, the boys in their mid-twenties, both were taller than their dad. And looking not much like their dad.

Don't go there, Andy. Not just now.

Chris was licking his lips nervously, and Dale was picking at his nose (when he thought no one was watching). And their guilty-faced mother Irina was half the time in the kitchen, hiding.

And finally at the end of the A W K W A R D meal when Irina was in the kitchen (of course!) under the pretext of cleaning up Chris turned this wincing smile on me and said in a croaking voice: "Dad, I think we should talk . . ."

And Dale chimed in, jumpily: "Yes, Dad. I th-think we should . . ."

And calm Dad smiled at them, and said: "So? Talk."

Had to laugh at their flushed faces, anxious eyes.

How gravely they took themselves. And each would've been thousands of dollars in debt except that their indulgent parents paid for their overpriced university educations, including even post-graduate training courses, without a murmur of complaint.

And now, their devious adulterous mother had summoned them behind my back.

If there's one thing a man hates, it is subterfuge within the family.

"Chris, if it's another loan you need, just tell me. I've never turned you down yet, have I?"

Chris was the older by two years. Just slightly deeper in debt than Dale. Spoiled brat with a face like a young Brad Pitt stared at me as if I'd slapped that face and for a moment his mouth worked with no words coming out.

"I—I didn't come for a loan, Dad . . . I—we—came to talk to you about some things Mom has been telling us."

Chris glanced at Dale who was gazing stonily at something on the table before him, rubbing his nose.

My tone was gently chiding, bemused—"Really! And what has 'Mom' been telling you two?"

"That—that—your drinking has gotten worse, Dad. That—"

"—you're angry with her all the time, and you've threatened her—"

Still Dad was not to be goaded into losing his temper.

"'Threatened her'—indeed, how?"

"Mom says you've grabbed hold of her, you've shoved her . . ."

"She says you lose your temper when you've been drinking and that your drinking has escalated . . ."

"'Escalated' isn't that a pretty big word! Sons? And where's the proof behind these charges?"

"Mom told us . . ."

"Mom said . . ."

Dad raised his voice, to summon Mom: "Hey 'Mom'! C'mon in here, 'Mom'! There are serious charges being levied against 'Dad.'"

"Dad, you're drunk right now. Jesus!"

"Dad, don't yell at Mom like that. You—you can't yell at Mom like that . . ."

"Can't I? Who in hell owns this house?—this property?" *Who is in charge here?* "Mom!" "MOM!"

Wisely, Irina stayed away. Might've fled to another part of the house.

"Dad, you're goddamn *drunk*. That's what we came to talk about—"

"What's this, some kind of crap 'intervention'? The family ganging up against the father? Who planned this?"

"Dad, we're not against you. We just want to, to—"

"—want to see if something is w-wrong—"

"—in your life, if—"

"—if something is—"

"Look, sons." (Very calmly, even affectionately, I enunciated *sons*. No one could confuse such solicitude with mockery, or fury.) "Your mother is the one who is emotionally unstable these days. Women her age—you know . . . 'Menopausal.' And she's exhausting herself at that damned Quaker school that pays in moral superiority instead of decent salaries, her and her left-wing liberal colleagues, the worst bigots—there's the *escalation*. Ask her! Interrogate her! Prosecute her! And I am *not drunk*."

It was true, I'd been drinking only white wine at the table. Only white wine, so far as the boys knew.

Too bad you don't have a firearm in this house.

The boys would never disrespect their father if he was properly armed.

Pushed back my chair. Managed to stand, and to exit the room with dignity.

Of course, they called after me—"Dad? Hey—Dad . . ."

Of course, they followed after me—"Dad? Please, we just want to talk . . ."

And Irina as well, following after me, but at a careful distance—"Andrew? Darling, please . . ."

Outside, and in the Jaguar. Out to get some air.

You don't love them, that's bullshit.
Never did, and you know it.
Given up enough for them, Mr. Nice-Guy.
Now—it's your turn.

And then—I saw!—a bicyclist traveling in the same direction in which I was traveling, on East Elm Road. And no witnesses in sight.

It was Huang Lee. Immediately I knew. Lanky, long-limbed, in a Friends School maroon sweatshirt (Irina had one just like it), wearing a shiny yellow crash helmet. As I approached him, pressing my foot on the gas pedal in quick increments, I could see, or begin to see, his flat Asian face—as he turned his head, glancing back over his shoulder, suddenly aware of danger—but too late.

God damn your soul to hell. All of you.

30　Hit and Run

"My God. No."

Even as the bicyclist turned his head, I'd seen—my brain had registered—this was not an adult male but a teenager—Asian features, jet-black hair visible beneath the shiny yellow helmet—dark eyes widened in terror—*not Huang Lee*. Yet, it was too late: the Jaguar sped into the bicyclist, into a tangle of flailing human limbs, screams, a clatter of metal against metal as the bicycle crumpled beneath the lethal weight of the car . . .

Limp as a rag doll the boy was flung onto the side of the road. Abruptly as he'd begun screaming he ceased screaming.

A thin line of red beneath the shiny yellow helmet, trickling out onto the pavement. Thin line of red that would become a gushing stream within seconds—if anyone had remained to observe.

31   Change of Venue

Next morning, I telephoned my agent in New York City.

That is, the longtime agent of Andrew J. Rush.

Quickly repeating the words I'd memorized, as if to forestall emotion.

"I—I've decided to retire, Barney. I won't be finishing this final novel. It's been too much for me, frankly. I don't even have a title, after nearly a year."

Barney was astonished. He'd known "Andy Rush" for more than thirty years—always the optimist, perennially good-natured—what was this?

"Which novel is this, Andy?—*Criss-Cross*? Isn't that the title?"

"No. It has no title. I never thought of a title."

"But, Andrew, we should discuss this. Have you told anyone else?"

"No."

But then I thought, *yes*.

"You don't actually sound like yourself, Andy. Are you—ill? Has something happened out there?"

Out there was my New York City friend's way of speaking of quasi-rural New Jersey. A tone of very gentle derision, which ordinarily I would counter with a witty wisecrack about the frenetic pace of the city, prohibitive price of real estate, trendy deafening restaurants. But today, Andy Rush was silent.

"Andy? Have you talked this over with Irina?"

"Irina isn't here right now, Barney. I'm going to hang up."

"Wait! Where is Irina?"

"I said—Irina isn't here right now, Barney. If you want to speak to her, that's between you and her."

"Andy, what does that mean? Are you and Irina—separated?"

"I'm going to hang up, Barney. Please don't call back."

"Andy, for God's sake let me come out to see you—I'll take a train today. Afternoon? Is that good for you? Around four P.M. Andy?"

Just hang up. And don't answer when he calls back.

Just delete the e-mails. Barney will catch on.

Spent much of the day in my writing room sketching out the next several Jack of Spades novels. These will be set in exotic locales with classy cinematic backgrounds: Tangier, Lisbon, Haiti, Amalfi coast of Italy, or maybe Sicily. Shanghai?

Since Jack of Spades has exhausted his interest in New Jersey a change of venue is prescribed.

Very exciting! My fingers are flying on this keyboard, my heart is racing.

These Jack of Spades novels will combine some of the intricacies of plot of A. Rush with the crude, quick-moving, visceral power of Jack of Spades. *Blend DNA of Stephen King, Mickey Spillane, Clive Barker, Jack Ketchum, Chuck Palahniuk plus sheer gut-wrenching carnage* . . . Euphoria swept through me like flame.

32   Auto-Erasure

This morning, I have made my decision.

Staring appalled at the photograph of seventeen-year-old Benjamin Chang in the newspaper: *hit-and-run Friends School senior bicycling home on East Elm Ridge Road, in critical condition at New Brunswick hospital. No witnesses have come forward.*

The only way to rid the world of Jack of Spades is to rid the world of Andrew J. Rush.

"He must be stopped. *I must be stopped.*"

It must be Catamount Park. The quarry, the boulders above the deep water, the high diving board.

A perfect circle.

Dearest Irina,
   Remember me as I was when you loved me.
   Please know—I have never ceased to love you.
   I am leaving you & the children for I am a danger to you.

* * *

If you are reading this, I am already departed.
You know the details of my will, you are my executrix.
I will leave specific instructions in this envelope.

I want to say—I am not to blame.
And yet—I am to blame.
Please forgive me!

Your loving husband
Andrew

It is remarkable how much time there is, in an empty house.

Time spreads out to fill a large vacuum-space.

More than enough time for me to draft letters to the Harbourton authorities confessing to the ax-slaying of C. W. Haider and the theft of the precious books; and to the "hit-and-run" of Benjamin Chang. More than enough time for me to take down the purloined books from my shelves and place them, with the purloined *The Glowering,* on a table close by in plain sight.

In the envelope for Irina I will leave checks—$500,000 each—made out to Esdra Staples and Benjamin Chang. I will explain to Irina the purpose of these checks and beg her to honor my request, which I have no doubt she will do.

God knows, this is a small enough reparation.

Stop! Are you insane? You are bluffing.

A stupid futile ploy of Andrew J. Rush. A desperate attempt to wrest the ending of the story from Jack of Spades . . .

The badly dented Jaguar will remain in the garage, no longer in use. It has become a vehicle of shame which (I seem to know) Irina will quickly sell.

The little silver flask is filled, for the final time.

That's it—take a drink! Two drinks.

A little whiskey to clear a muddled brain.

But the clearer the brain, the more adamant I am about the matter of *auto-erasure.*

At Caramount State Park, I have parked my station wagon in at the entrance to the swimming quarry. On this chilly day in early spring the park is deserted.

A sky so vivid-blue my eyes well with tears.

It is a farther hike to the quarry than I recall. Already I am short of breath as I begin to climb above the quarry, making my crab-like way across the clay-colored misshapen boulders (defaced now with graffiti), not so easy for me at fifty-four as it was at twelve, the last time I was here.

Don't be sentimental! You don't give a damn for your dead brother, in fact you've forgotten his face.

There, the makeshift diving board. It seems hardly to have changed over the years.

But not so high above the water as I recall. Fifteen feet? Twelve?

An icy crust on the dark water like an eyelid shielding an eye.

What are you doing? Are you crazy?

Are you play-acting? Is that what this is?

I have weighed the numerous pockets of my nylon jacket and my khaki pants with large stones. I have laced up heavy hiking boots that tug at my ankles like weights. Very carefully I climb the metal rungs to the top of the ladder, and very carefully I make my way along the diving board. How cold the air is, suddenly! And not so still as it had seemed on the ground.

A stab of panic, that I might be blown off-balance by a gust of wind, and fall into the freezing-dark water, before I am prepared . . .

So many years have passed, and Evan has been dead all these years while I have been alive.

"I'm sorry, Evan. Whatever I did, or imagined doing, has been a shadow across my life."

Bullshit. You resented your younger brother, and you pushed him off the diving board.

Maybe you didn't want him to die but—he died.

I will step off the end of the diving board and I will fall straight down, arms flat against my sides. I will fall straight down, feet first.

Swift and sharp as a blade entering the water, disturbing the thin icy crust.

With just a few startled ripples, I will sink into the deep water. But no one will cry out, having seen.

The boy! He isn't swimming, he's sinking . . .

Somebody get help for him—the boy . . .

At the end of the diving board I am standing very still. A blackness comes over my vision, I am not seeing clearly. I have begun to shiver with cold and with the almost unbearable excitement of what is to come.

"There is no other way. This is the right decision."

To destroy evil we must destroy the being which evil inhabits, even if it is ourselves.

I think that I will die of the sudden shock for I am no longer twelve years old. I am fifty-four, and my heart has sometimes hurt, like a muscle in spasm. I have told no one about this for I have been ashamed of my mortality and I have been frightened of what the very word *mortality* means. I will die of icy-cold water pressing against my chest, my face, my eyes. If I am fortunate the shock will cause me to lose consciousness within seconds. Like any desperate drowning creature I will gasp for breath but it will be water I will take into my lungs.

You won't. You will not. To kill me, you must kill yourself. And you are weak, a coward. You will not.

At the very end of the high diving board. There is movement here, a just-perceptible movement of the board, a faint creaking beneath my weight. Above, the sky is so blue, my eyes are pierced. I am standing very still, very tall with my shoulders erect and my head high. In my pockets are heavy stones. Nylon jacket, khaki pants. Jack of Spades has been observing with disdain and mockery and yet he understands now that I am serious and his laughter turns harsh, incredulous. *You can't. You won't. God damn your soul to hell, YOU WILL NOT.*

But I am breathing deeply now, with conviction. I feel the movement, light as a breath, of someone or something close behind me.

Hairs stir on the nape of my neck, in an ecstasy of anticipation. I do not turn, and I do not flinch, as the fingers gently touch me and urge me out into the air